THE ROVER BOYS OUT WEST OR THE SEARCH FOR A LOST MINE

By

ARTHUR M. WINFIELD

double9
books

The Rover Boys Out West;
Or
The Search For A Lost Mine
by **Arthur M. Winfield**

ISBN: 978-93-57273-12-1

Published by

DOUBLE 9 BOOKS

2/13-B, Ansari Road, Daryaganj
New Delhi – 110002
info@double9books.com
www.double9books.com
Tel. 011-40042856

ABOUT THE AUTHOR

Arthur M. Winfield (Edward Stratemeyer) was born on October 4, 1862, to Henry Julius Stratemeyer a tobacconist, and Anna Siegel. He was an American publisher, writer of Children's fiction, and founder of the Stratemeyer Syndicate. He was probably the most creative author in the world, producing over 1,300 books and selling over 500 million copies. He also created many famous fictional book series for juveniles, including The Rover boys, The Bobbsey Twins, Tom Swift, The Hardy boys, and Nancy Drew. As a teenager, Stratemeyer worked at his own printing press in the basement of his father's tobacco shop, distributing flyers and brochures to his relatives. These included stories titled The Newsboys Adventure and The Tale of a Lumberman. After graduating from high school, he worked in his father's shop. He is not even 26 in 1888 while Stratemeyer sold his first story Victor Horton's Idea, to the famous children magazine The Golden Days.

CONTENTS

INTRODUCTION

My Dear Boys: This book, "The Rover Boys Out West," forms the fourth volume of the "Rover Boys Series," a line of up-to-date stories for Young Americans. Like the other books of the series, this tale's complete in itself.

In "The Rover Boys at School" we were introduced to Dick, Tom, and Sam, and their amusing and thrilling adventures at Putnam Hall, a military academy for boys situated in the heart of Now York State; in "The Rover Boys on the Ocean" we followed our young heroes during a most daring rescue; and in "The Rover Boys in the jungle" we learn what true American courage can do, even in the heart of the Dark Continent.

In the present tale our young herm are taken at first back to dear old Putnam Hall, and then to the heart of the great mining district of Colorado.

All trace of a valuable mine has been lost, and the boys start out on a hunt for the property, little dreaming of the many perils which await them on their quest. How they overcome one obstacle after another, and get the best of their various enemies, will be found in the story itself.

The success of the first Rover Boys books has gratified me beyond measure, and my one hope is that my numerous readers will find this and future volumes of equal interest.

Affectionately and sincerely yours,

ARTHUR M. WINFIELD.

June 20, 1900

CHAPTER I
RETURNING FROM A GREAT GAME

"Zip! Boom! Ah!"

"Hurrah for Putnam Hall!"

"Let her go, Peleg, lively now, and mind you don't upset us, or we'll use you worse than we did the football."

"All right, young gents. All in? Hold fast, everybody, or I won't be responsible, nohow, if you drop off. Git along, Jack; up with ye, Sally!"

And with a crack of the whip, a tooting of tin horns, and it mad yelling and cheering from the students, the long Putnam Hall stage left the football enclosure attached to the Pornell Academy grounds and started along the lake road for Putnam Hall.

The stage was packed, inside and out, with as merry and light-hearted a crowd of boys as could be found anywhere; and why should they not be merry and light-hearted, seeing as they had just won a great football match by a score of 16 to 8? Tom Rover, who was on the top of the stage, actually danced a jig for joy.

"That's the third time we have done them up, fellows!" he cried. "My, but won't there be gloom around Pornell Academy to-night! It will be thick enough to cut with a knife."

"They were never in it from the start," piped up Sam Rover. "And they were all heavier than our team, too," he added, proudly.

"It was science, not weight, that won the match," said Frank Harrington.

"Yes, it was science," broke in Larry Colby. "And for that science we have to thank Dick Rover. Oh, but didn't that rush to the left fool them nicely!"

Dick Rover's handsome face flushed with pleasure. "We won because every player did his full duty," he said. "If we—" He broke off short. "Great Scott, what a racket on top! Who's that capering around?"

"It's me, thank you!" yelled Tom, with more force than good grammar. "I'm doing an Indian war dance in honor of the victory. Want to join in, anybody?"

"Stop it; you'll be coming through the roof. We had only one man hurt on the field; I don't want a dozen hurt on the ride home."

"Oh, it's safe enough, Dick. If I feel the roof giving way I'll jump and save myself," and Tom began a wilder caper than ever. But suddenly George Granbury, who sat nearby, caught him by the foot, and he came down with a thump that threatened to split the stage top from end to end.

"It won't do, nohow!" pleaded Peleg Snuggers, the general utility man attached to Putnam Hall Military Academy. "Them hosses is skittish, and—"

"Oh, stow it, Peleg," interrupted George. "You know those horses couldn't run away if they tried. You only want us to act as if we were a funeral procession coming—"

A wild blast of horns from below drowned out the remainder of his speech, and this finished, the football team and the other cadets began to sing, in voices more forceful than melodious:

"Putnam Hall! Putnam Hall!
What is wrong with Putnam Hall?
Nothing, boys! Nothing, boys!
She's all RIGHT!
Right! right! Right! Right! RIGHT!"

Through the woods and far across the clear waters of Cayuga Lake floated the words, followed by another blast from the horns and then continued cheering. And their cheering was answered by others who passed them, some in carriages and others oil bicycles. It was a clear, sunshiny day, and nearly all of the inhabitants of Cedarville, as well as of other villages along the lake, were out in honor of the occasion. It had been a general holiday both at Putnam Hall and at Pornell Academy, and the whole neighborhood had taken advantage of it.

"I believe Captain Putnam is as proud as any of us," remarked Dick Rover, when the excitement had calmed down a bit. "When Tom kicked that final goal I saw him rise up and nearly pound the life out of the railing with his gold-headed cane. I'll wager the cane is split into a dozen pieces."

"Oh, that's nothing," put in Harry Blossom slyly. "When Tom did his little act I saw Nellie Laning actually throw him a kiss from the grand stand. If she—"

"Hi, below there! Who's taking my name in vain?" came from Tom, and suddenly his head appeared at the top of one of the openings on the side of the stage.

"I was just telling what Nellie Laning did, Tom. When you made that splendid kick—"

"Stow it, you moving-picture camera!" cried Tom, his face growing suddenly red. "You see altogether too much."

"Do I?" drawled Harry dryly. "Maybe. And then when Dick made his run, pretty Dora Stanhope just put out her arms as if she wanted to hug— Whow!"

Harry Blossom's banter came to a sudden ending, for, as red in the face as his brother, Dick Rover reached forward and thrust a banana he was eating into the tormenter's half open mouth. Harry gulped once or twice, then the fruit disappeared as if by magic.

"All right, Dick, I accept the bribe and will henceforth be silent," he said solemnly, as soon as he could speak.

"That's right, tie up your tongue, unless you want to be lifted from the stage," said Tom.

"It's all right," put in Dave Kearney, another cadet. "Dora Stanhope and the Laning girls are nice folk and I don't blame anybody for being sweet on them."

"Yes, but you keep out of their cornfield, or you'll have all three of the Rovers after you," came from Harry warningly.

"What are we going to do to-night?" asked Dick abruptly, and in such a tone that the others felt the bantering must come to an end. "Is it feast, or fireworks, or both?"

"Make it both!" came in chorus from a dozen cadets. "Captain Putnam is just in the humor to let us do anything to-night. And Mr. Strong's in the same good humor. Let us make the best of it."

"All right; feast and fireworks it is," said Dick. "But both will cost money. Who'll pass around the hat?"

A groan went up, as is generally the case when an academy boy is asked to part with some of his spending money. But the groan counted for nothing, and the passing of the hat brought in over ten dollars.

"Ten-sixty for this load," announced the cadet who had made the collection. "And there are two other loads following, besides those who were on their wheels. We ought to be able to collect at least thirty dollars, and that will buy out half of Cedarville."

"If only old Carrick has some of his Fourth of July fireworks left," said Sam.

"Chust so!" grinned Hans Muelle, the German cadet who had joined the academy the season before. "Vot is von celebration midowit firevorks, hey? He vos chust noddings!"

"Do you want another pistol explosion?" asked one of the others, referring to an incident between Tom Rover and Hans which had nearly ended in a tragedy.

"Mine cracious, no!" howled the German lad. "I go me not py a hundred feet mid an old pistol again alrietty! I vould radder sit town on von can of dynamite to sleep, yes I vould!" And he shook his curly head earnestly.

"We won't have any pistols in this," broke in Tom, who felt like shuddering every time the incident was mentioned. "We'll just have skyrockets, and Roman candles, and pin-wheels, and all of the rest of the good old-fashioned things—that is for the celebration on the outside."

"And for the celebration on the inside let us have cake, ice-cream, fruits, and nuts," put in Larry. "At this minute I feel hungry enough to eat the captain out of house and home."

"Ditto myself," came from another student.

"Perhaps the captain will be glad enough to have us celebrate—at our own expense," suggested a cadet in one corner, yet he did not mean what he said, knowing that bluff Captain Putnam, the owner and headmaster of Putnam Hall was whole-souled and generous to the core.

The stage had already covered over a mile of the road, and now the turnout left the lake shore and began to climb a long hill leading to the heights upon which the academy was located. But there was still a little valley to cross, at the bottom of which dashed a rocky mountain torrent on its way to the placid waters beyond.

At the top of the first long rise Peleg Snuggers stopped the team for a few minutes' rest. Here the view was magnificent, and many a cadet stopped his idle talk to gaze at the mountains to the westward and the sparkling lake winding along in the opposite direction. It was early fall, and nearly every tree was tinted with red and gold, while here and there the first frosts had covered the ground with leaves and nuts.

"Don't wait too long, Peleg," urged Tom impatiently. "It will take some time to get ready for our celebration to-night, you know."

"I'm hurrying as fast as I can, Master Tom," was the reply. "Git up, Jack! git up, Sally!" And once more they moved off, and again some of the boys tooted their horns. At this Sally picked up her ears and gave a little start to one side of the narrow road, dragging her mate along.

"Whoa! Steady there!" cried Peleg Snuggers, and tried to pull the team in. Failing in this He grabbed the brake handle and pushed it back vigorously. He was so nervous that he gave the handle a mighty wrench, and in a twinkle the brake bar snapped off, close to the wheel. Onward bounded the stage, hitting the team in the flanks, and away leaped both horses on a dead run!

"The brake is broke!"

"Stop the team, Peleg, or they'll upset us sure!"

"Whoa, there, Jack! Whoa, Sally! Don't you know enough to stop?"

Such were some of the cries which rang out. Peleg Snuggers grasped the lines and pulled with might and main. But then came an awful bump, and away flew the driver into a bush along the roadside, and the reins fell to the horses heels, scaring them worse than ever.

"We are in for it!" gasped Tom. "I don't see how we are going to stop them now."

"The bridge! The bridge across the gully!" screamed another cadet, in terror-stricken tones. "They were mending it this morning. Supposing they haven't the new planking down?"

"There is the bridge!" burst out another, pointing ahead. "Oh, Heavens, boys, we are lost!"

All strained their eyes ahead to see what he meant, and then every face grew pale. The bridge was torn up completely, not a single plank of the flooring remained.

CHAPTER II
SOMETHING ABOUT THE ROVER BOYS

The Rover boys were three in number, Dick being the oldest, Tom coming next, and Sam the youngest. In their younger days they had resided with their parents in New York, but after the death of their mother and the disappearance of their father they had gone to live with their uncle, Randolph Rover, and their Aunt Martha, on a farm called Valley Brook, near the village of Dexter Corners, on the Swift River.

Those who have read the previous volumes of this series, entitled respectively, "The Rover Boys at School." "The Rover Boys on the Ocean," and "The Rover Boys in the jungle," know that our three heroes had already passed through many trying experiences and thrilling adventures. From home they had been sent to Putnam Hall, a military academy of high standing, and here they had made many friends, including those already mentioned, and several enemies, among the latter being one Dan Baxter, who was known as the school bully, and John Fenwick, better known as Mumps, the bully's toady. They had also made a bitter enemy of Josiah Crabtree, the headmaster of the Hall.

But since those first days at the school many things had happened and many changes had occurred. It was discovered that Dan Baxter was the son of one Arnold Baxter, a rascal who had, years before, tried to swindle the Rover boys' father out of some valuable mining property in the West, and that the son was little better than his parent. Dan had left the school in a hurry, and soon after this his father had been arrested in Albany for a daring office robbery, and was now in jail in consequence.

The disappearance of Dan, and Josiah Crabtree's yearning for wealth, had led to further complications. Near Putnam Hall resides the widow Stanhope and her pretty daughter Dora, and Crabtree, who exerted a sort of hypnotic power over the widow, tried to get the lady to marry him, so that he might obtain the fortune she held in trust for her daughter. But how the Rover boys fooled the grasping teacher, and how Dora was saved from the plot Crabtree and Dan Baxter hatched up against her, has already been told in "The Rover Boys on the Ocean."

Anderson Rover had gone to Africa to locate certain mines in that country, and when many years passed and no word came from him the three boys grew worried and wanted to go in search of him. At last came a strange letter written by a sea captain, containing some important information, and acting on this the Rover boys, accompanied by their Uncle Randolph, set out for the heart of the Dark Continent to find the long-lost. On the way they fell in with one Alexander Pop, who had formerly been a waiter at Putnam Hall, who proved a valuable friend when it came to dealing with men of his own ebony hue. In this hunt they likewise ran across Josiah Crabtree, who was out with an exploring party from Yale, and with Dan Baxter, and both of these rascals tried to do them much harm. But the schemes of the rascals fell through, and Crabtree only escaped after a severe whipping at the hands of Dick Rover, while Dan Baxter fared little better. Soon after this Mr. Rover was found, as a prisoner of a savage African tribe, and rescued, and then the entire party returned to the United States. Alexander Pop remained in the employ of the two elder Rovers, and the three boys returned to finish the term at Putnam Hall.

These are a few of the things that had happened. But there were countless others, which space will not permit being mentioned here. There had been many contests, in baseball, football, and other sports, and jokes that seemed to have no end, and there had also been a disastrous fire, which none of the Putnam Hall cadets were likely ever to forget—a fire as thrilling as the scene now being enacted on the road. But I am afraid I have already left the boys in the runaway stage too long, so we will return to them without further delay.

"The bridge is down!" The cry rang through the stage, bringing every cadet to his feet on the instant.

"Don't jump!" cried Dick, as he saw several preparing to leap. "You will break your necks!" For now the bushes were left behind, and on either side of the road were jagged rocks, covered here and there with withered vines.

As Dick spoke he pushed his way to the front of the stage and crawled out on the driver's seat.

"The back—drop off at the back!" came from Frank Harrington, and he showed how it could be done. But the road was now rougher than ever, and he landed on his knees and his face, giving himself an ugly cut on the chin.

Dick was trying to reach the reins when Tom came down beside him.

"Can you make it?" asked Tom.

"I can try," was the desperate answer. "If only we could block those wheels!"

"Block the wheels!" came from half a dozen, and one boy, who happened to have a stout cane with him, thrust it out between several of the spokes of the wheel on the left, in the rear. For an instant the stick held, then it snapped, and the wheel went around as before.

The bridge was now less than two hundred feet away, and whatever was to be accomplished must be done quickly. At last Dick had the reins, and he began to pull upon them with all of his strength, at the same time calling upon Tom to hold him to the seat.

"To the right—turn 'em to the right!" sang out Sam, as he saw a narrow opening between the rocks.

"Yes, the right!" added Fred Garrison. "It is our only hope!"

Dick did as requested, and at the last instant the heavy stage swung around. There was a grinding and a splitting of wood as the front wheels met the rocks and went to pieces, and then Dick came down on the horses, with Tom on top of him—and the elder Rover knew no more.

"Dick's hurt!" gasped Sam, as he scrambled out of the side window of the turnout. "Don't let the horses kick him."

For the runaway team were struggling wildly, amid the rocks and the wreck of the harness. But Tom was already up, and he and Larry Colby dragged Dick to a place of safety. In the meantime some of the other cadets who were used to managing horseflesh took care of the team and led them away and tied them fast to a tree.

"Dick, Dick! are you badly hurt?" The question came from Tom, as he gazed anxiously into his brother's face. There was a nasty cut on the left check from which the blood was flowing.

Dick did not answer, and Tom asked somebody to run down to the stream for some water. When this was brought he and Sam bathed Dick's face, and presently the latter opened his eyes and stared around him in bewilderment.

"A touchdown—I claim—" he began, and then stopped. "Wha— what has happened?" he stammered. "Oh, I remember now!" And he feel back again.

"He thinks he's still in the football game," whispered Harry Blossom. "Oh, but he's a plucky one."

All of the other lads had been severely shaken up, but nobody had been hurt excepting Frank, as before mentioned. Soon he came limping up, followed by Peleg Snuggers.

"I missed it by jumping," he observed ruefully. "Hullo, is Dick knocked out?"

"So ye stopped 'em, eh?" cried the general utility man. "It was prime plucky to do it, so it was! Poor Dick, hope he ain't bad."

By this time Dick was opening his eyes once more, and this time he kept them open.

"I—I—that was a nasty tumble, wasn't it?" he muttered. "I'm glad I didn't go under the horses' feet."

"How do you feel?"

"I guess I had the wind knocked out of me, that's all." He tried to get up, but his legs refused to support him. "I'll have to keep quiet awhile."

"Yes, don't you move," said Sam. "We can't get across the stream anyway, now the bridge is down. We'll have to go around to the other bridge."

"It's queer the workmen didn't put up some sort of a sign as a warning," said Fred Garrison. "I believe they can be held liable for this disaster."

"To be sure they can be held liable," burst out Peleg Snuggers.

"But a sign wouldn't have kept the brake from breaking," said Tom.

"True, lad, but ye must remember that it was their duty to put the sign up at the beginning of this road, which is on the top of the hill. If the sign had been there we would never have started to come down this way."

"Perhaps we missed the sign," put in another cadet.

"Of dot is so, ve besser run pack und stop udder carriages from comin' dis vay," broke in Hans Mueller quickly. "Listen to dot!"

They all listened, and heard merry cries of laughter and carriage wheels rapidly approaching.

"A carriage — with ladies!" gasped Sam. "Come on and stop them!" And away he, dusted up the hill, as well as his short legs would carry him. Hans, Larry, and several others followed. They had barely gained the top of the hill when a large carryall belonging to John Laning appeared. In the carryall were the farmer and his two charming daughters, and, Mrs. Stanhope, who was his sister-in-law, and her daughter Dora. Mrs. Laning was also present, along with several neighbors.

"Hi, whoa! stop!" yelled Sam. "Stop!"

"Hurrah for Putnam Hall!" cried Grace Laning, waving a tiny flag toward Sam, which made the younger Rover blush.

"Glad to be able to congratulate you, Sam!" said Dora Stanhope. "Where are the other members of the football team?"

"Just ahead — down by the gully. You mustn't drive down here, for the bridge is down."

"Bridge down!" ejaculated John Laning. "Darwell said he was going to mend it this week, but I saw no sign up at the cross-roads."

"Neither did we, and we came near to going overboard. As it is, we had a pretty bad smash up!"

"Indeed!" came from Mrs. Stanhope, in alarm. "And was anybody hurt?"

"Dick was thrown out and knocked unconscious, and Frank Harrington had his chin cut, while the rest of us were pretty well shaken up. Peleg the driver was thrown into some brushwood and that most likely saved his life."

Mrs. Stanhope grew pale, for she remembered only too well that fateful ride she had once taken with Josiah Crabtree, which had almost cost both of them their lives.

"I will go to the poor boy!" she said, and leaped to the ground, followed by Dora and the two Laning girls. Soon the carryall was led to the side of the road, and the others alighted, to see what damage had been done.

CHAPTER III
THE MISSING DANGER SIGNAL

When Sam came back he found Dick sitting on a rock with his cut plastered up from the out kit taken along to the football match. Frank had likewise been attended to.

"I am so glad you are not hurt seriously," said Mrs. Stanhope, as she sat down beside Dick, with Dora close at hand. "All of you have had a very narrow escape."

"It is a shame that no danger signal was display," said Dora. "When they are fixing a bridge they usually put a bar across the road with the sign: 'Danger! Road Closed,' on it."

"Exactly," put in Peleg. "But I haint seen no sign, an' that I can swear to."

"In that case Contractor Darwell will be responsible for this smash up," said John Laning. "Are the horses hurt?"

"They are pretty well scratched up around the legs."

"Humph! And the two front wheels of the stage are a total wreck. I reckon it will take the best part of fifty dollars to fix matters up."

"Anyway, I don't calculate as how I'm responsible," grumbled the general utility man, fearing he saw trouble ahead, when Captain Putnam should hear of the affair.

A creaking on the road was heard, and presently a lumber wagon hove into sight, piled high with the new planking for the bridge. On the front sat Darwell the contractor and two of his workmen.

"Hullo, what does all this mean?" cried the contractor, as he brought his wagon to a standstill, and viewed the wrecked stage.

"It means that Captain Putnam will have a little account to settle with you, Mr. Darwell," put in Harry Blossom promptly.

"With me? What for?"

"For this wreck."

"And for this cut chin," added Frank.

"And my being knocked out," said Dick.

"I'm not responsible for any wreck," replied Joel Darwell. "I put up the bar with the danger signal on it, up at the cross-roads."

"We didn't see no sign," interrupted Peleg Snuggers. "Not a bit of a sign."

"There was no sign when I came along," said John Laning.

"I put the sign up not over three hours ago," insisted Joel Darwell. "I can show you just where Sandy Long and I dug the post holes for it."

"Then some rascal took the sign down," said Tom. "What for?"

"Must have done it to wreck the stage," answered Larry Colby. "But could anybody be so cold-blooded?"

"Yes, there are several people who would do that," answered Dick promptly. "But I don't think they are within a hundred miles of Cedarville just now."

"You mean Dan Baxter for one," said Sam.

"And Josiah Crabtree for another," put in Tom. "They are both down on everybody around here."

"How about Mumps?" asked Larry.

"Oh, he reformed after that chase on the ocean, and I've heard he is now out West," said Sam. "There's another rascal, though—Mr. Arnold Baxter. But he is in jail in Albany—he and that tool of his, Buddy Girk."

"Well, certainly somebody is responsible," said Frank. "Supposing we go back and try to find some clew?"

"And find the danger sign and put it up again," said Joel Darwell.

A dozen of the boys went back, and with them Tom and Sam, leaving Dick with the Stanhopes. As soon as the crowd had left, Dora Stanhope motioned the elder Rover to one side.

"Oh, Dick, it makes me shiver to hear Josiah Crabtree spoken of," she said in a whisper.

"Why, Dora, you don't mean to say that he has turned up again?" he questioned quickly.

"No—but—but—last night I heard a strange noise on our side porch, as if somebody was trying the side window. I went to the door and asked to know who was there. At once I heard somebody or some animal leave the porch and climb over the side fence of the garden. I am almost certain it was some person trying to get into the house."

"Did you tell your mother?"

"No, she had one of her nervous headaches, and I thought it would do no good. But I couldn't sleep all night, and I laid with a big stick in one hand and papa's old revolver in the other. The revolver wasn't loaded, but I thought I might scare somebody with it."

"The revolver ought to be loaded, Dora. Do you know what caliber it is?"

"No; you know I know little or nothing about firearms."

"Then I'll find out for you, and get some cartridges. If Josiah Crabtree is around you ought to shoot him on the spot."

"Oh, I couldn't do that—even though I do know how dreadfully he treated you while you were in the heart of Africa."

"You must be very careful of your movements, especially after dark. Crabtree may be around, with some new scheme against you or your mother. I wish he could have been left behind in Africa."

"Oh, so do I! but he and Dan Baxter both came back to America, didn't they?"

"So we heard in Boma. But don't get worked up too much, Dora, for it might have been only a cat,—or a common tramp looking for something to eat. We have had lots of tramps around the Hall lately."

"I have asked Grace Laning to pay us a visit, and she is coming over to-morrow."

"Then you will have somebody in the house besides your mother and yourself. I wish I could stay with you folks."

"How long are you going to remain at the Hall, Dick? When you came back you said something about going out West with your father to look up that mining claim in Colorado."

"We shan't start for the West until next spring. Father was going right away at first, but after he found out that Arnold Baxter was safe in jail and couldn't bother him any more, he concluded to remain with Uncle Randolph and Aunt Martha until next spring so as to give himself the chance to get back his old-time strength. His sufferings in Africa pulled him down a good bit."

"I suppose. Well, I am glad you will be around during the winter. Next summer mamma has promised to go with me on a trip to Buffalo and then around the Great Lakes. I trust the lake air will do her much good, and that we won't hear or see anything of Mr. Crabtree while we are on the water."

"I'd like to go with you on that trip," answered Dick. "I have no doubt you will have a grand time."

Little did he dream of all the perils that trip was to lead to, and of how he and his brothers would be mixed up in them.

In the meantime the others had journeyed up the hill to where the road branched off in three directions. At this point Joel Darwell pointed out two newly-made holes in the earth, about fifteen feet apart.

"See them?" he cried. "Well, that is where I placed the danger sign, and I am willing to swear to it."

"And so am I," added the workman who was along.

"Well, there is no danger signal here now," returned Tom, glancing around. Some bushes torn up beside the road attracted his attention, and he hurried toward them. "Here you are!"

He pointed to a cleared spot behind the bushes and there, on the ground, lay the torn-up posts and boards. Evidently somebody had dragged them thither in great haste.

"It's the work of some thorough rascal!" cried Sam. "Somebody who meant mischief to our stage."

"Maybe dis vos der vork of dem Pornell Academy fellers," suggested Hans.

"No, they are gentlemen, not scoundrels," replied Tom. "They may feel cut up, but they wouldn't play such a dastardly trick as this."

The spot was one commanding a good view of the back road, so that anybody standing there could have seen the stage coming while it was still a quarter of a mile off.

All hands began a search for some clew leading to the identity of the evil-doers—that is, all but Joel Darwell and his helper. These two dragged the posts and boards into position again, and this time set them down so firmly that a removal would be out of the question without tools.

"Hullo, here's something!" cried one of the cadets presently. "Did you just drop this, Tom?"

As he spoke he held up a round, flat coin of coppery metal, engraved with several circles and a rude head.

"No, I didn't drop it," replied Tom, his face growing serious. "Did you, Sam?"

Sam gave a look, placed his hand in his pocket and brought out a similar piece. "No, there is mine," he said. "Where in the world did that come from?"

Then Tom and Sam looked at each other. The same idea crossed the mind of each. The coin was similar to those they had handled while on their way through Africa. They had brought home several as pocket-pieces.

"I'll wager Dan Baxter dropped that!" cried Tom. "He, or—"

"Josiah Crabtree!" finished Sam. "Yes, I am sure of it, for Dick brought none to Putnam Hall; I heard him tell the Captain so, when they were talking about coins one day."

"Then in that case, either Baxter or Crabtree is responsible for this smash-up!" came from one of the other cadets.

"Right you are. The question is, which one?"

"Perhaps both vos guilty," suggested the German student.

"That may be true, Hans," came from Tom. "I wonder if one or the other of the rascals is in hiding around here?"

"We'll begin a search," said Sam. "Hans, go and call the others," and at once the German cadet started off on his errand.

CHAPTER IV
A TRAIL IS FOUND AND LOST

By this time several carriages had come up, also a number of folks on bicycles and on foot, and to all of these the situation had to be explained. Among the last to put in an appearance was Captain Putnam, and he was at once all attention, and desired to know how seriously Dick and Frank were injured.

"It was an outrageous piece of work," he said.

"Still, to be fair, we must admit that the broken brake is largely responsible for what happened, after the start down hill was made."

"But I couldn't help the brake breaking," pleaded the general utility man. "I did my best, and was thrown out—"

"I am not finding fault with you, Snugger," cut in the captain, shortly. "Let it pass, and leave the stage to be taken care of by the Cedarville blacksmith. But I wish we might lay hands on the rascal who is responsible for the start of the mishap."

"They have found a coin such as we used when as we were in Africa," said Dick. "I think that furnishes a clew."

"In what way, Rover?"

"Those coins were also used by Dan Baxter and Josiah Crabtree."

"And you think one or the other, or both, are in this neighborhood again?"

"It looks plausible, doesn't it?"

"Yes, but—it would be very strange. I should think they would give this locality a wide berth."

"Hardly. Josiah Crabtree isn't done with the Stanhopes, to my mind, and Baxter will get square with us if he can."

While this talk was going on Sam and Tom were following some footprints leading from the clearing where the signal board had been found down a small path toward the lake. The footprints were clearly defined.

"The prints are not very large," observed Tom, as he and his brother measured them. "It looks to me as if Dan Baxter's feet might have made them."

"Certainly they weren't made by old Crabtree," said Sam. "He had a very long foot and always wore square-toed boots."

They followed the prints down to the lake shore, and then along the rim of the lake for nearly half a mile.

Here there was a little cove, and under some bushes they discovered some marks in the wet dirt of the bank, as if a rowboat had been moored there. In this dirt the footprints came to an end.

"That's the wind-up of this trail," sighed Tom. "Water leaves no trail."

"That's so. But supposing we skirt the lake some more."

They went on, and did not give up until the declining sun told them the day was done.

When they reached the Hall they found that all of the others had come in, and that preparations were already going forward for the feast in the evening. For once Captain Putnam and George Strong, his main assistant, were going to allow the cadets to have their own way. Secretly the captain was tremendously pleased over the showing his pupils had made on the football field, for this happened to be a year when college athletics were in the ascendancy in all of the States.

But the regular evening drill must not be neglected, and soon the sound of the drum was heard, calling the members of companies A and B to the parade ground. A rush was made for uniforms, swords, and guns, and soon the boys come pouring forth, Dick as a captain, and his two brothers as under officers.

"Attention!" shouted the major of the command. "Forward! march!"

"Boom! boom! boom, boom, boom!" went the drums, and then the fifers struck up a lively tune, and around the academy marched the two companies at company front. Then they went around again by column of fours, and then marched into the messroom, where they stacked arms and sat down at the long mess tables. The movements were patterned after those at West Point, and could not have been improved upon.

"Well, what of the hunt," asked Dick, as soon as he got the chance to talk to Tom.

"We followed it to the lake and then lost the trail," answered his brother. "But I am convinced that the rascal was Dan Baxter."

"I believe you are right, Tom," answered Dick, and related what Dora Stanhope had told him. Of course Tom listened with keen interest.

"We made a mistake in letting old Crabtree and Baxter go when we had them in Africa. We should have handed them over to the authorities."

"I am not worried about Baxter so much," went on Dick. "But I hate to think of Crabtree being around to molest the Stanhopes."

"And especially Dora," grinned Tom.

"Right you are, Tom, and I am not ashamed to admit it to you. But please don't—don't well, make fun of it to me any more."

"I won't, Dick." Tom gave his brother's hand a squeeze under the table. "Dora is all right, and if some day I get her for a sister-in-law I won't complain a bit." This plain talk made Dick's face flush, but he felt tremendously pleased, nevertheless, and loved Tom more than ever.

Directly after supper the boys were given until eleven o'clock to do as they pleased. At once some old barrels were piled high at one end of the campus, smeared with tar, stuffed with wood, and set on fire, and the blaze, mounting to the sky, lit up the neighborhood to the lake on one side and the mountains on the other.

Four cadets had gone down to Cedarville to buy the fireworks and the things to eat, and by nine o'clock these returned, loaded down with their purchases. Among the crowd was Larry Colby, who sought out Dick as soon as he arrived.

"I've got news," he exclaimed. "Whom do you suppose I saw down in Cedarville? Josiah Crabtree!"

"You are certain, Larry?"

"Yes."

"Where did you meet him?"

"Down at the restaurant where he went for some ice cream. He was just paying for a lunch he had had when I came in."

"Did you speak to him?"

"No; I wanted to do so, but as soon as he saw our crowd coming in he dusted out of a side door."

"Was he alone?"

"Yes."

"Humph!" Dick's brow clouded. He was inclined to think that Dora had been right concerning the noise she had heard on the side porch.

"You haven't any idea where he went?"

"No; I wanted to follow him, but it was dark on the street and he slipped me."

This was all Larry had to tell, and he hurried to arrange the fireworks.

The celebration was a grand success, and lasted until almost midnight. The boys had brought along a lot of Roman candles and skyrockets, and these they set off from the top of one of the tallest trees on the grounds.

"So that the Pornell fellows can see them," said Sam. "I know they will enjoy the show," and then he closed one eye suggestively. The Pornell players had chaffed him on account of his size, and now that the victory was won, he did not mean to let them forget their defeat too quickly.

At about ten o'clock Dick went to Captain Putnam and asked permission to leave the grounds for an hour or two.

"Where do you wish to go?" asked the captain.

"To Mrs. Stanhope's, sir," and he related what Dora had told him, and of what news Larry Colby had brought.

"I am afraid you may get into trouble, Rover," said the captain seriously.

"I will be very careful, sir. I am not afraid of Mr. Crabtree, should he turn up."

"I don't believe you are afraid of anyone," said the master with a smile, for he admired Dick's courage.

"Then you will let me go?"

"Wouldn't you rather have somebody with you?"

"I wouldn't mind having Tom along."

"I meant some grown person—like, for instance, Mr. Strong."

"No, sir."

"Well, then, take Tom. But mind and be careful, and don't stay too late if everything is right, down there."

Having received this permission, Dick hurried to Tom. Soon the two brothers were on the way, Tom eating some cake and peanuts as they hurried along. The latter hated to miss the feast, but did not wish to see his brother under take the mission alone.

It was a clear night, and although there was no moon, the stars twinkled overhead like so many diamonds. Both knew the short cut to Mrs. Stanhope's cottage well, and made rapid progress. "Shall you ring the bell if everything appears to be right?" asked Tom, as they came in sight of the modest dwelling, set in the widow's well-kept garden.

"I guess not, Tom. It's so late. Both Mrs. Stanhope and Dora have probably gone to bed."

They had almost reached the gate to the garden when Dick caught his brother by the sleeve and drew him back into the shadow of a large maple tree.

"What is it, Dick?"

"I think I saw somebody moving around the corner of the house just now."

Both boys strained their eyes, but could see nothing that resembled a human form.

"I don't see a thing, Dick."

"Come, we'll move around to the outside of the garden," returned the older brother.

The flower garden was not large, and was separated from the vegetable laths. As they made their way along this, both caught the sound of a window sliding up.

"Hark! Did you hear that?" whispered Dick excitedly.

"I did. It came from the back of the house."

"Somebody must be trying to get into the kitchen window!"

Dick broke into a run, with Tom at his heels. Entering the garden by a rear gate, they soon reached the vicinity of the kitchen. A window stood wide open, and through this they beheld somebody inside the apartment with a blazing match in his hand trying to light a candle.

"Hi, there, who are you?" cried Tom, before Dick could stop him.

At the sound of the call the man in the kitchen jumped as though stung by a bee. Then he wheeled around, with the lighted candle in his hand, and both boys saw that it was Josiah Crabtree.

CHAPTER V
A STRUGGLE IN THE DARK

"Crabtree, you rascal!" ejaculated Dick.

"Who—who is that?" spluttered the former teacher of Putnam Hall, in dismay.

"It is I—Dick Rover. What are you doing here?"

"I—I came to call upon the Widow Stanhope," stammered Josiah Crabtree. He was so astonished he knew not what to say.

"You came to rob her, more likely," sneered Tom. "You just broke in at the window."

"No, no—it—it is all a mistake, Rover. I—I am stopping here for the night."

"Indeed!" gasped Dick, almost struck dumb over the man's show of "nerve," as he afterward expressed it.

"Yes, I am stopping here."

"With Mrs. Stanhope's permission of course."

"Certainly. How could I stop here otherwise?"

"What are you doing in the kitchen all alone?'"

"Why, I—er—I was up in my room, but I—er—wanted a glass of water and so came down for it."

"Then Mrs. Stanhope and Dora have gone to bed?"

"Yes, they just retired."

"Have you become friends again?" asked Dick, just to learn what Josiah Crabtree might say.

"Yes, Rover, Mrs. Stanhope is once more my best friend."

"Then she doesn't know what a rascal you were out in Africa."

"My dear Richard, you are laboring under a great delusion. I was never in Africa in my life."

"What!" roared Dick aghast at the man's audacity.

"I speak the truth. I have made an investigation, and have learned that somebody went to Africa under my name, just to take advantage of my—ahem—of my exalted rank as a professor."

"Great Scott! how you can draw the long bow!" murmured Tom.

"I speak the plain truth. I can prove that for the past six months I have been in Chicago and other portions of the West.

"Well, if you are a guest here, just stay with Tom while I call the Stanhopes," said Dick, and leaped in at the window.

"Boy, you shall do nothing of the kind," cried Josiah Crabtree, his manner changing instantly.

"Why not? If you are friends, it will do no harm."

"Mrs. Stanhope is—er—is not feeling well, and I will not have her disturbed by a headstrong youth like you."

"We'll see about that. If you—"

Dick broke off short, for just then a voice he knew well floated down into the kitchen from upstairs.

"Who is talking down there? Is that you, Dick?" It was Dora speaking, in a voice full of excitement.

"Yes, Dora, it is I—and Tom. We have caught Josiah Crabtree here in your kitchen."

"Oh!" The girl gave a little scream. "What a villain! Can you hold him?"

"We can try," answered Dick. He turned to Crabtree. "I reckon your game is up, old man."

"Let me go!" growled the former teacher fiercely, and as Dick advanced upon him he thrust the lighted candle full into the youth's face. Of course Dick had to fall back, not wishing to be burnt, and a second later the candle went out leaving the room in total darkness.

But now Tom sprang forward, bearing Crabtree to the floor. Over and over rolled the pair, upsetting first a chair and then a small table.

At the sound of the row Dora Stanhope began to scream, fearing one of her friends might be killed, and presently Mrs. Stanhope joined in. But the cottage was situated too far away for any outsiders to hear, so the boys had to fight the battle alone.

At length Josiah Crabtree pulled himself clear of Tom's hold and made for the open window. But now Dick had recovered and he hurled the man backward.

The movement kept Crabtree in the room, but it was disastrous to Tom, for as the former teacher fell back his heel was planted on Tom's forehead, and for the time being the younger Rover lay stunned and unable to continue the contest.

Finding himself unable to escape by the window, Josiah Crabtree felt his way to the door and ran out into the hall. Because of his former visits to the house he knew the ground plan well, and from the hall he darted into the parlor and then into the sitting room.

Dick tried to catch him, and once caught his arm. But Crabtree broke loose and placed a large center table between them.

"Don't dare to stop me, Rover," hissed the man desperately. "If you do you will be sorry. I am armed."

"So am I armed, Josiah Crabtree. And I call upon you to surrender."

"What, you would shoot me!" cried the former teacher, in terror.

"Why not? Didn't you try to take my life in Africa?"

"I repeat, you are mistaken."

"I am not mistaken, and can prove my assertion by half a dozen persons."

"I have not been near Africa."

"I won't argue the point with you. Do you surrender or not?"

"Yes, I will surrender," replied Josiah Crabtree meekly.

Yet he did not mean what he said, and as Dick came closer he gave the lad a violent shove backward, which made the elder Rover boy sit down in an easy chair rather suddenly. Then he darted into a small conservatory attached to the sitting room.

"Stop!" panted Dick, catching his breath.

"Tom, he is running away!"

Crash! jingle! jingle! jingle! Josiah Crabtree had tried the door to the conservatory and finding it locked and the key gone, had smashed out some of the glass and leaped through the opening thus afforded.

By this time Dora was coming downstairs, clad in a wrapper and carrying a lamp in her hand. The first person she met was Tom, who staggered into the hall with his hand to his bruised forehead.

"Oh, Tom, are you hurt?" she shrieked.

"Not much," he answered. "But Dick—Dick, where are you?"

"Here, in the conservatory. Crabtree just jumped through the glass!"

Dora ran into the little apartment, which Mrs. Stanhope had just begun to fill with flowers for the coming winter. Tom came behind her, carrying a poker he had picked up.

"Is he out of sight?" asked Tom.

"Yes, confound the luck," replied his brother. "Which way did he go?"

"I don't know."

"We ought to follow him."

"We will." Dick turned to Dora. "After we are gone you had better lock up better than ever, and remain on guard until morning."

"I will, Dick," she answered.

The key to the conservatory door was hanging on a nearby nail, and taking it down they unlocked the door, and the two boys passed into the darkness of the night outside.

"Please take care of yourselves!" cried Dora after them, and then turned to quiet her mother, who had come downstairs in a state of excitement bordering on hysteria, for, as old readers know, Mrs. Stanhope's constitution was a delicate one.

Running into the garden, Dick made out a dim form in the distance, on the path leading to the lake.

"There he is!" he cried. "Come, Tom, we must catch him, if we can!"

"I am with you," answered Tom. "But take care what you do. He may be in a desperate frame of mind."

"He is desperate. But I am not afraid of him," returned the elder Rover, with determination.

Josiah Crabtree was running with all the speed of his long legs, and the two lads soon found that they had all they could do to keep him in sight.

"Stop!" yelled Tom, at the top of his voice, but to this command the former, teacher paid no attention. If anything, he ran the faster.

"He is bound for the lake," said Dick. "He must have a boat."

But Dick was mistaken, for just before the water came into view Josiah Crabtree branched off onto the road leading into Cedarville. Then of a sudden the shadows of a patch of woods hid him from view.

"He's gone!" came from Tom, as he slackened his speed.

"He didn't turn down to the lake."

"That's so. He must have gone toward Cedarville."

The Rover boys came to a halt and looked about them searchingly. On one side of the road lay a tilled field, on the other were rocks and trees and bushes. They listened intently, but only the occasional cry of a night bird broke the stillness.

"We are stumped!" groaned Dick dismally.

"What, you aren't going to give up the hunt already, are you?" demanded Tom.

"No, but where did he go?"

"Perhaps he went back to the house."

"I don't believe he would dare to do that. Besides, what would he go for?"

"What made him go in the first place?"

"I am sure I don't know. Perhaps he was going to abduct Dora — or Mrs. Stanhope."

"If he was going to do that alone, he would have had his hands full."

The two boys advanced, but with great caution. They peered into the woods and behind some of the larger rocks, but discovered nothing.

"That is the second time we have lost our game to-day," remarked Tom soberly. "First it was Dan Baxter or somebody else, and now it is Josiah Crabtree."

"It must have been Baxter who tried to wreck the stage. He and old Crabtree always did hang together."

"If they are stopping anywhere in Cedarville we ought to put the police on their track."

"I'll do that sure. We can easily hold both on half a dozen charges — if we can catch them."

CHAPTER VI
AN INTERESTING LETTER

But to catch Josiah Crabtree was not easy. The former teacher of Putnam Hall was thoroughly alarmed, and once having taken to the woods, he plunged in deeper and deeper, until to find him would have been almost an impossibility. Indeed, he completely lost himself, and when the boys had left the vicinity he found himself unable to locate the road again, and so had to remain in the cold and damp woods all night, much to his discomfort. He could not keep warm, and sat chattering on a rock until daylight.

Finding it of no use to continue the search, Dick and Tom retraced their steps to the Stanhope homestead. They found Dora on guard, with every window and door either locked or nailed up. The girl had persuaded her feeble mother to lie down again, but Mrs. Stanhope was still too excited to rest comfortably.

"Did you catch him?" Dora asked anxiously, after she had admitted them.

"No, he got away in the darkness," answered Dick.

"It is too bad. What do you suppose he was up to?"

"That is what we would like to find out, Dora. Certainly he was up to no good."

"Perhaps he wished to rob us."

"He must know that you do not keep much money in the house."

"Day before yesterday mother had me draw four hundred dollars out of the bank, to pay for the new barn we have had built. The carpenter, however, went to Ithaca on business, so as yet we have not been able to pay him the money."

"It was a mistake to keep so much cash in the house. You should have paid by check—it's the same thing," put in Tom.

"I know it, but Mr. Gradley is peculiar. He once had some trouble over a check, and he stipulated that he should be paid in cash."

"Do you suppose Josiah Crabtree saw you draw the money from the bank?" remarked Dick thoughtfully.

"I don't know what to think."

"He would be just rascal enough to try to get it, if he knew of it. I guess we had better remain here until morning, and after that you had better have a man around the house."

"Yes, mother says she will hire a man. But men are difficult to get—that is, one who is reliable. We had to discharge Borgy on account of drunkenness."

"Perhaps father will let Alexander Pop come up here for a while," cried Dick, struck with the idea. "I don't believe he needs the man at home, and Aleck is thoroughly reliable, even if he is colored."

"Yes, I know Pop well. I would like to have him first-rate. But it is asking a good deal at your hands, Dick."

"As if I wouldn't do a good deal more than that, Dora," he cried quickly, and caught her hand.

"I know you would—you have already. You are the best friend I have, Dick—you and your brothers."

"And I always will be, Dora, always!" he whispered, and pressed her hand so tightly that she blushed like a peony.

Tom had passed into the kitchen and was looking around to see what damage his struggle with Crabtree had done. Nothing was injured. Under the kitchen table lay a letter and a small vial. He picked up both.

"Chloroform!" he cried, as he smelt of the contents of the vial, just as the others came in.

"Where did you get that?" asked Dora.

"Found it under the table, along with this letter. Crabtree must have dropped both."

"Let me see the letter!" cried Dick.

Tom passed it over, and all three read the communication with interest. It had been sent to Josiah Crabtree while the latter had been stopping in New York, and was post-marked Albany.

"It's from Dan Baxter," said Dick.

The letter ran as follows:

"Dear Mr. Crabtree:

"I drop you a few lines as promised. I have seen my father and his plans are about completed. The Rovers think they have the upper hand, but when he gets out of jail he will be able to show them a thing or two and surprise them. If you go to Cedarville I will meet you there on the 5th of next month—at the old meeting place. We won't have Mumps, the turncoat, to bother us, and maybe we can lay plans for a fat deal all around. Anyway, we ought to square accounts with those Rover boys. They treated both of us outrageously and they ought to suffer for it.

"Yours as faithfully as ever,

"**D.B.**"

"Won't Crabtree be mad when he finds out that he lost this?" grinned Tom.

"He may not know that he dropped it here."

"Well, it clears up one point. Baxter and he are both around, and intent on mischief."

"True enough."

"What shall you do next?" put in Dora anxiously.

"I hardly know. 'Forwarned is forearmed,' they say, but Baxter and Crabtree are such underhanded rascals one never knows what to expect of them next."

"Of course you will tell the Cedarville police—or I shall."

"I'll do that. But you know what they did before. Never helped us a bit, but let both slip through their fingers."

"Perhaps they will be on their mettle now."

The situation was talked over for half an hour, and then it was decided that Tom should return to Putnam Hall to explain to Captain Putnam and to Sam, while Dick should remain with the Stanhopes.

This agreed upon, Tom took his departure immediately, as it was now midnight, and he did not wish to be locked out for the night.

"And now you had better return to bed, Dora," said Dick, after his brother had departed. "I will remain downstairs, on the sofa, and I don't believe anybody will disturb me."

"All right, if you wish it that way," replied the girl. "But you can have one of the bedrooms if you wish."

"No, I'll stay here, and keep my clothes on."

Dora went upstairs, but soon came back, carrying a pillow and a quilt.

"There, that will provide a little comfort," she said, but then, as Dick caught her hand as if to kiss it, she gave a merry little laugh and ran upstairs again.

It was a long while before Dick could go to sleep. He had read the letter found in the kitchen with care, and he wondered what it all meant.

"What plans can Arnold Baxter be completing?" he asked himself. "And how can he surprise father? Can that refer to the missing mine in Colorado? He talks as if he was going to get out of jail pretty soon, but that can't be, for the judge will certainly give him three or four years at the least. Perhaps I had better write to father about this."

No other person came that night to disturb the inmates of the cottage, and when at last Dick did fall into slumber he did not awaken until the sun was shining in the window and a neighboring Irish woman, who did Mrs. Stanhope's washing and ironing, was knocking on the kitchen door for entrance.

"Good-morning, Mrs. O'Toole," he said, as he leaped up and let her in.

"Good-marnin', young sir," stammered the washerwoman. "Sure an' I didn't ixpict to see you here."

"I suppose not. But come in, and I will call Miss Dora."

"No need to call me, if you please," came in a silvery voice from the hall, and Dora appeared, as bright and fresh as ever. "I would have been down before, only I had to wait on mamma."

"And how is she?"

"She is no worse, but neither is she better. I shall send for our doctor to-day."

Breakfast was soon on the table-fresh coffee, fresh eggs, and dainty buckwheat cakes baked by Dora's own hands. It is needless to say that Dick enjoyed the repast.

"You'll make a famous housekeeper for somebody some day, Dora," he said, looking at her pointedly.

"You go and eat your cakes before they get cold," she answered.

"I've already eaten my fill, I can't go another one. I've enjoyed them ever so much. Now I guess I had better be off for Cedarville."

"If you wish, you can hitch up Dolly to the carriage and drive over. It will be nicer than walking."

"Supposing I go over on horseback? Is she used to a saddle?"

"Oh, yes, and you will find a gentleman's saddle in the harness closet back of the stalls."

"Then I'll go that way. Good-by. I'll be back before noon, unless something unusual turns up. And when I am down in Cedarville I'll send word to father about Aleck."

Leaving the house Dick went to the barn, which was usually locked. Dora had given him the key, but to his surprise he found the padlock pried off and the door partly open.

"Can this be more of Crabtree's work?" he asked himself. "Perhaps he has stolen the mare! What fools we were not to look in here last night."

But Dick's fears were groundless. The mare was still there. But she was all saddled, ready for him to ride.

"Crabtree's work, beyond a doubt," he thought.

Before he went to the house he came here, and it was his intention to steal the mare and get away on her.

CHAPTER VII
A HUNT THROUGH THE WOODS

Before starting for Cedarville Dick acquainted Dora with the discovery he had made.

"We were fortunate," said the girl. "I would not lose Dolly for a good deal."

If there was one thing Dick loved it was a good horse, and once on Dolly's back he urged the little mare along at top speed. She was in prime fettle, and flew along the hard road as if she thoroughly enjoyed the outing.

Arriving at Cedarville Dick sought out the little police station, for the town had at last taken on a force, consisting of a chief and eight men.

The chief, a little fat man by the name of Burger, sat in his office reading the Cedarville Trumpet, the weekly journal of the place.

"Want to see me on business, eh?" he said, laying down the sheet. "All right, young man, sit down. What name?"

"Richard Rover. I am one of the cadets at Putnam Hall."

"Just so. Trouble at the Hall, I presume? Anything connected with that celebration last night?"

"No, sir, I—"

"Another robbery, then? Captain Putnam seems to have his hands full."

"We've had no robbery at the Hall, sir. I came—"

"No robbery, eh? Then perhaps it's a fight. Students will fight when they get celebrating. I know we had a fight once at the academy I attended, and it lasted three days."

"I hope they called out the fire department," answered Dick, with a grin.

"The fire department—Ha! ha! a good joke! No; they called in the doctor, ha! ha! So it's a fight, eh? Does the captain want us to arrest anybody?"

"It's not a fight."

"What? But you said—" The fat chief paused.

"I said I wanted to see you about business."

"Just so—and that you were from Putnam Hall, and Captain Putnam had sent you."

"No, no. Please give me a chance to talk."

"Why, of course. I never interrupt anybody. Go on, but don't take too much time, for my time is limited."

"I came from Mrs. Stanhope's cottage, man broke in there last night—"

"Ha, a burglary! Why didn't they let us know at once? Or perhaps you have collared the villain already?"

"No, we haven't got him, although my brother and I tried to catch him."

"Pooh! Two boys, and tried to catch a burglar! Of course he got away."

Dick felt disgusted, and arose to make his departure.

"If you won't listen to what I have to report, I'll take myself off," he said half angrily.

At this Chief Burger stared at him in astonishment.

"Really, you are a remarkable boy," he gasped. "Ain't I listening to everything you are saying?"

"Hardly. I wish to tell you everything from the beginning."

"Just so. Go on, I shan't say a word. What a remarkable boy! But it must be the military training that does it."

As well as possible Dick told all that had happened during the night. Chief Burger interrupted him a score of times, but at last the tale was finished. At the conclusion the chief closed one eye suggestively.

"And don't you know where this Josiah Crabtree is now?" he asked.

"If I did I'd go after him hot-footed," returned Dick.

"He must be in hiding in the woods near the cottage."

"Perhaps, but he had eight hours in which to get away."

"Just so. I will send out an alarm to all of my force, and then Detective Trigger and I will make a personal hunt for the rascal."

"When you hunt for him you had better hunt for Dan Baxter, too," said Dick, and he told of the happening on the stage ride.

"I will keep an eye open for Baxter, too," said the chief.

From the police station Dick rode to the post office, and here wrote and mailed a long letter to his father, relating what had happened and repeating the wording of the letter that had been found. He requested that Alexander Pop be sent up without delay.

There was nothing to keep Dick in Cedarville any longer, and he prepared to return to the Stanhope cottage with the mare. But before going he entered the leading drug store, and here purchased a box of choice chocolates for Dora, for he fortunately had his spending money with him, or at least the balance left over from the football celebration.

When Dick reached the cottage he found both the washwoman and the carpenter at work, one in the wash-house and the other finishing up the new barn. The money taken from the bank had been turned over to Mr. Gradley, so Mrs. Stanhope no longer had this to worry her.

Feeling that he could do little at school for the balance of that day, Dick resolved to hunt through the woods for some trace of Josiah Crabtree, and went off shortly after giving Dora the chocolates, over which the girl was greatly pleased. He followed the road in the direction of the lake at first, and was about to plunge into the brushwood when a distant voice hailed him.

"Hullo, Dick, stop! I want to see you."

It was Sam calling, and soon his youngest brother came up on a run.

"Sam, what brings you?" he asked, for it was easy to see that something out of the ordinary had occurred.

"I want to know where Tom is," panted Sam.

"Tom?" Dick's face grew pale all in an instant. "Didn't he return to Putnam Hall last night?"

"No, and nobody around there has seen him since he went off with you. I thought he was with you, until Dora just told me that he started to return about midnight."

"He did. And he didn't return? What can it mean?"

"What's the trouble here?"

Sam was given the particulars, and uttered a long, low whistle.

"That looks black, doesn't it?"

"It does, Sam. I don't like it for a cent."

"Do you suppose he fell in with Crabtree?"

"Perhaps—or with somebody just as bad."

"Perhaps he spotted Crabtree and started to follow him."

"I shouldn't think he would follow him all this time without letting somebody know."

For several minutes the two brothers discussed this new turn of affairs. Both were greatly troubled, and Dick did not know whether to continue his hunt or not.

"I wouldn't care if only I knew he was all right," he said.

"That's just it. Tom is able to stand up for himself in an even fight, but if Crabtree played him some trick—"

"Let us hunt for him," interrupted the elder Rover. "There is no use of our sitting down and sucking our thumbs."

They went along the road until the spot was gained where Josiah Crabtree had been last seen. Then they began a systematic search until Sam discovered what he said were fresh footprints leading directly into the woods. At one point one of the prints was very plain, and they saw that it was made by a long shoe, square-toed.

"I reckon you have struck it, Sam," said Dick, after an inspection. "Now if only we can stick to the trail to the end."

Fortunately the ground was so damp that the trail could be followed with ease. An hour's walking brought them to the rock where the former teacher had spent the larger part, of the night.

"He made a stop here, that's certain," observed Dick, as they surveyed the criss-cross tracks.

"Like as not he got mixed up in the dark, Dick. It must have been awfully black here under the trees."

Presently they discovered another trail, leading up a hill. Beyond was a tall tree which Josiah Crabtree had climbed in order to obtain a better view of the surroundings. From the tree the trail led directly toward the lake.

"We're on his track, all right enough," observed Sam. "But if he took to the water we'll lose it, just as we lost Baxter's trail yesterday."

The trail crossed the main road and came out at the lake where there was a slight bluff covered with a heavy growth of underbrush. To their right was an old building, which in years gone by had been a dwelling.

"There is a fire over yonder," observed Dick, as he pointed past the building "Somebody seems to be burning a lot of wet brush. See the heavy smoke."

"Perhaps the folks at the fire can tell us something of Crabtree," answered Sam. "Let us go over and interview them."

His brother was willing, and as well as they were able they pushed their way through the brush toward the fire.

The latter burned fiercely, and presently the two boys detected the odor of tar.

Then they reached a point where they could overlook what was going on around the fire, for the blaze was located in something of a gully of the cliff.

"Merciful heaven!" burst from Dick's lips, and he stood spellbound. Sam also gave a look, and the sight that both boys saw nearly froze the blood in their veins.

CHAPTER VIII
WHAT BECAME OF TOM

To go back to Tom at the time when he left Dick and the Stanhopes, and started to return to Putnam Hall.

He went away whistling gayly, for he thought that all danger was over.

"What a shame I had to miss the celebration," he murmured. "And after my success on the football field, too!"

Soon the Stanhope grounds were left behind, and he struck the main road leading to the academy.

He had advanced a distance of several hundred feet along this road when, on looking ahead, he observed some person coming slowly toward him.

Wondering who the individual could be, and thinking of Crabtree, he stopped short.

At the same time the other person also halted, and then of a sudden slipped out of sight behind the nearest trees.

"Hullo, that's queer," murmured the youth. "Evidently he doesn't want to be seen. Can it be Crabtree?"

He was unarmed, and had some hesitancy about advancing, not knowing what to expect.

But he did not wish the former teacher to escape, and so casting around he espied a sharp stone and picked it up.

"Hi, there, come out of that!" he called, as he ran forward and held the stone ready for use.

No reply was vouchsafed, and he called again. By this time he was directly opposite the spot where the mysterious individual had disappeared.

"Look here, Josiah Crabtree, you might as well come out and give yourself up," he called sharply.

Still there was no answer, and now Tom did not know what to do. Under the trees it was so dark that he could scarcely see a yard in front of him.

Yet he advanced several paces, still holding the stone up as a weapon of offense or defense, as the case might prove. But nobody appeared in sight, and at last he returned to the road.

He was in a quandary whether to return to the cottage or continue on his way to the Hall.

"I suppose I may as well go on," he concluded. "Neither Dick nor I can do much in the woods in the dark."

So he went on, but this time more slowly, wondering if Josiah Crabtree would follow him, and never dreaming that the person who had slipped him was not the former teacher, but Dan Baxter.

For Baxter it was, who had been waiting around to be joined by Crabtree, for the pair of evil-doers had come to the vicinity of the Stanhope cottage together.

"It's Tom Rover," muttered Baxter, on hearing the boy's voice. "I was lucky to get out of the way."

He remained as motionless as a statue while Tom passed within a dozen feet of him. Then When Tom went out on the road again Baxter ran forth, too, but in the opposite direction.

Down on a side road Baxter had that day run across a tramps' encampment. In the camp were three hoboes, as they are sometimes called rascals who were willing to do almost anything but work for a living.

They had demanded money of the bully, and he gave them a dollar, fearing violence if he refused them.

Baxter now thought of the tramps, and as he did so an evil look crossed his face.

"If only I can pay off Tom Rover," he muttered. "I'll do it if I can."

Soon the tramps' encampment was reached, and he found two of the men dozing before a tiny fire, with an empty liquor bottle between then the third tramp had gone to Cedarville for more liquor.

"Wake up here," cried Baxter, catching first one and then the other by the shoulder.

"What do yer want, young feller?" demanded the leader of the party, who rejoiced in the name of Stumpy Nuggs.

"I want you two men to help me lay a boy out," answered Dan Baxter, feeling that there was no use in mincing matters, for he knew that the tramps were a bad crowd.

"Lay a boy out?" repeated the second tramp, who was called Longback.

"Yes, he is an enemy of mine, and just passed on the road yonder. If you will help me thrash him and make him a prisoner, I'll give you each five dollars."

"Say, yer talkin' big," said Stumpy Nuggs.

"I mean what I say. I know you are not above doing such work by the way you tackled me."

"Is de boy alone?"

"Yes."

"An' yer want to whip him and den make him a prisoner?"

"Yes."

"Wot yer goin' ter do wid him after dat?"

"I don't know yet."

"Who is de boy?"

"A cadet up at the military academy above here."

Stumpy Nuggs scratched his head of tangled hair.

"Maybe yer gittin' us into a trap fer askin' yer fer dat dollar," he observed suspiciously.

"No, I am not. This boy is an old enemy of mine, and I want to get square with him. We can easily catch him before he gets to the academy, if you hurry up."

"An' you will give us five dollars each?"

"Yes—and perhaps more. The boy carries a watch, and must have some money in his pocket. He also wears a gold ring."

At the mention of jewelry and money the tramps' eyes glistened.

"If you are tellin' de truth, dis is all right," cried Stumpy Nuggs, as he arose and stretched himself.

"I am telling the truth, and you can easily prove it for yourselves. Only hurry up, or it will be too late."

The two tramps consulted together, and asked a few more questions. Then they agreed to follow Baxter, and do whatever he desired of them, providing they were allowed their fair share of plunder, if there was any.

In the meantime Tom went on in deep thought. He still held the stone in his hand. He wished he had a club, but the stick he had formerly picked up had been left at the cottage.

The hall grounds had just come into sight in the dim distance when the boy heard the patter of footsteps behind him.

He turned around, but could see nobody, and at that instant the sounds ceased.

"Somebody is following me," he thought. "Can it be the same party I spotted before?"

An instant later he found himself confronted by two men and a boy, each with a bit of cloth tied over his face, into which two holes had been cut for eyes.

"Is dat him?" asked one of the men.

"Yes," answered the boy, in a strangely unnatural voice. "Give it to him."

All three of the party carried sticks, and they at once fell upon Tom, hitting him over the shoulders and the head.

He did his best to defend himself, and hit Baxter in the arm with the stone, inflicting a wound that made the bully shriek with pain.

"So it is you, Baxter!" cried Tom, recognizing the voice. "What do you mean by this?"

"Knock him down," yelled the bully. "Don't let him get away from you!"

Thus urged, the two tramps closed in, and while one caught Tom by the arm, the second tried to pull his feet from under him.

It was a fierce, but unequal struggle, and though the boy struck out right and left, inflicting not a little injury, in the end he found himself on his back, with Stumpy Nuggs sitting on his chest.

"You rascals, let up," he gasped. "Do you mean to kill me?"

"Lay still, or you'll catch it worse," growled Nuggs. "Where's dat rope, Longback?"

A rope had been brought along, and it was quickly produced, and then Tom was rolled over and his hands were bound behind him. His legs were also bound together in such a fashion that he might walk but not run.

"Now get up," ordered Dan Baxter, with a wicked scowl.

Not caring to remain on the ground, Tom did so. He noted that the two men with Baxter were tramps, and he came to the conclusion that he had a hard crowd with whom to deal.

"March!" went on Baxter, taking Tom by the shoulder.

"March? Where to?"

"You'll find out fast enough."

"Suppose I refuse."

"You had better not, Tom Rover. You know I'm not to be trifled with."

"I am not afraid of you," answered Tom boldly. "You were always a bully, Dan Baxter, and a bully is a coward."

"Is your name Baxter?" asked asked Stumpy Nuggs, curiously.

"Never mind what it is," growled Baxter.

"I used ter have a friend wot knowed a feller named Baxter," went on the tramp. "Me friend's name was Buddy Girk."

"I know your friend," cried Tom. "He once stole my brother Dick's watch. He is this boy's father's tool, and both of them are now in jail in Albany for robbery."

"Wot!" cried Nuggs, in astonishment. He turned to the other tramp. "Longback, I reckon we have struck an odd crowd, hey?"

"Dat's wot," answered Longback. "But say, we didn't go through de young gent's pockets yet."

"Wait until we are off the road," interrupted Dan Baxter. "Somebody may come along and make trouble for us."

"Right ye are," answered Stumpy Nuggs. "Don't let's stay here anudder minit."

With Baxter on one side of him, Nuggs on the other, and Longback bringing up the rear, Tom was forced to march along. Once he resisted, and received a punch in the side that took nearly all of the wind out of him. He started to cry for help, but his captors threatened if he did this that they would place a gag of dirty cloth in his mouth.

In days gone by Baxter had often visited a deserted dwelling on the lake shore, and to this spot the party now directed their steps. In the dark their course was uncertain, and they made slow progress, so it was after three o'clock in the morning when the dilapidated building was reached.

CHAPTER IX
A DOSE OF TAR AND FEATHERS

"Make some kind of a light—I can't see a thing," said Dan Baxter, as the little party came to a halt in front of a half tumbled down building.

Stumpy Nuggs carried matches, and quickly lit a bit of candle which he produced from one of the pockets of his ragged attire.

They entered the dwelling, forcing Tom to accompany them. This done they tied the young cadet fast to an iron ring set in the huge old fashion fireplace.

"Now we'll turn out his pockets," said Longback, and this was quickly done. To the tramps' chagrin Tom carried no watch, but had with him two dollars in money.

"Now we'll take dat ring," said Nuggs, pointing to the article on Tom's little finger.

"So I have fallen in with a lot of thieves, eh?" said the boy. "Well, if you want the ring you can fight for it."

"Shut up!" roared Dan Baxter, and struck him across the mouth, causing Tom's under lip to bleed. The boy tried to retaliate, but his bonds held him fast.

While one tramp held his hand the other possessed himself of the ring. The ring contained an opal of which Tom was very proud, and to part with the article made the young cadet feel pretty bad.

"You will rue this night's work," he muttered. "I'll see you in prison for it."

"Don't waste your breath in threatening," cried Baxter.

"All right, Baxter, wait and see. I'll put you where your father is."

The bully's face reddened. "Will you shut up, or do you want another crack on the mouth?"

"It's only a coward who would strike a person when he is helpless."

"Coward or not, I want you to keep a civil tongue in your head."

"Perhaps you imagine we don't know who tried to wreck the stage," went on Tom pointedly.

"Wreck a stage? I know nothing of such a thing."

"You know all about it. And we'll prove it too—when you are under arrest."

"I won't talk to you!" howled Baxter.

"Come with me," he added to the tramps, and then the three quitted the building, leaving Torn to his reflections, which were dismal enough.

"I'm in a pickle and no mistake," he murmured. "What will they do with me next?"

Hour after hour went by and still Tom was left alone. In the meantime Baxter had held a long conversation with the tramps and had formed a compact with them, paying them the ten dollars as agreed.

The sun was shining brightly when at last Dan Baxter re-entered the old building.

"Getting hungry, I suppose," he remarked, with a wicked grin.

"Not particularly so," answered Tom coldly. He was hungry, but he was not going to admit it.

"I suppose you would like to have your liberty," went on the bully.

"Don't ask superfluous questions, Baxter. Let us get down to business. Why did you make me a prisoner, and what are you going to do with me?"

"I made you a prisoner because I felt like doing so," growled the big youth.

"And what do you propose to do next?"

"Teach you a lesson that you won't forget all your life, Tom Rover."

"Thank you for nothing."

"I haven't forgotten how you and your brothers handled me out in Africa—and here, too, for that matter."

"You deserved what you got, Dan Baxter. Some persons would have had you sent to prison for your actions."

"Bah! You don't know what you are talking about. What were you doing out so late last night?"

"None of your business."

"Were you over to the Stanhopes' place?"

"Perhaps I was and perhaps I wasn't."

"Don't get mulish. Remember that you are absolutely in my power."

"And what if I was at the Stanhopes' place? Haven't I a perfect right to go there?"

"Did you meet anybody there?"

"Yes, I did. I met your particular friend, Josiah Crabtree."

Baxter's face fell. "And what—that is what did you have to say to each other?"

"Crabtree tried to rob the widow—and I believe you were outside waiting for him," Tom continued suddenly.

"Nonsense."

At this moment Stumpy Nuggs came in.

"There's a man comin' dis way!" he said excitedly, "Wot shall we do?"

"A man!" ejaculated Baxter, in alarm. "I'll go out and see if I know him."

He left the building with the tramp. The newcomer was approaching along the gully path. As he drew closer Baxter recognized Josiah Crabtree.

"Baxter!" exclaimed the former teacher, as, he carne up. "This is fortunate; I was afraid you had been captured."

"And I was afraid you were in the same box," rejoined Baxter.

"I had a hard time of it to get away. I got lost in the woods and had to remain out in the cold all night."

"Then you didn't succeed in getting what you wanted, or in seeing Mrs. Stanhope?"

"No. Those confounded Rover boys turned up, and I had to—ahem—leave in a hurry. But who are these two men?" and Josiah Crabtree looked apprehensively at the tramps.

"They are all right, Crabtree. They helped me do a slick thing last night."

"Ah, and what was that?"

"I met Tom Rover on the road and they helped me to capture him."

"Indeed, and where is the—ah—young rascal now?"

"A prisoner in the old house yonder."

At this information Josiah Crabtree was much astonished, and begged for the particulars of the affair, which were speedily forthcoming.

"And now you have him a prisoner, what do you propose to do?" asked the former teacher.

"I'll soon show you," growled Baxter. "I'm going to do him up brown—or rather, black. See here."

He led the way back to the gully and pointed to a pot of tar and a brush which rested by it.

"It is tar!" cried Crabtree.

"Exactly."

"And you are—ahem—going to give him a coat of that?"

"Yes. Doesn't he deserve it?"

"To be sure he does. I will assist you," answered the former teacher readily, with a malicious gleam in his fishy eyes. "I wish you had all three boys here, to tar them with the same brush."

"One at a time, Crabtree. We'll fix the others some time later."

A fire was started and the pot of tar was hung from a chain caught up between two uprights.

Some of the softening stuff was smeared on the wood which was burning, and this made the blaze more fierce than ever. Soon the tar was near to the boiling point.

The two tramps had thrown themselves down to watch the proceedings.

"Yer ought ter have some fedders," suggested Longback.

"I have. There was an old musty feather bed in the house. I'm going to use that."

Going into the building Dan Baxter brought forth the feathers in question, and placed them close to the pot of tar.

While he was doing this Josiah Crabtree went in to talk to Tom.

Of course the boy was surprised to see the former teacher, who eyed him darkly.

"So Baxter has caught you," began Crabtree.

To this Tom made no answer.

"I presume you do not like your present position," went on the man.

Still no reply.

"You feel so bad about it that you do not even Wish to talk, is that it?"

"No, I was just thinking of what an ugly, black-hearted villain you were, Crabtree," aid Tom, looking him full in the face. "I don't believe you have a single spark of honor left in you."

At this Crabtree's face grew as dark as a thunder cloud.

"Ha I how dare you address me in this fashion?" he cried.

"I know I am taking a great risk, but I cannot help it."

"Do you forget that you and your brothers are solely responsible for my present position? That but for you I would have married the Widow Stanhope and started one of the finest boys' school in New York State?"

"Yes, and you would have made Mrs. Stanhope perfectly miserable, and squandered every dollar that she holds in trust for Dora."

"That is your opinion, and it is worth nothing."

"My opinion is the opinion of everybody that knows you as well as I do."

"You have constantly interfered in the doings of myself and of others, and now you must stand punishment for the same."

"What do you intend to do?" demanded Tom quickly.

"I'll show you," broke in the voice of Dan Baxter, and he came in, followed by the two tramps. Soon Tom was released from the fireplace and marched between them out into the open air.

"How do you like that?" asked Baxter, as he led the way to the fire. "Tar and feathers are fine, aren't they?"

"You would tar and feather me?" asked Tom, and now it must be confessed that he shivered in spite of his efforts to remain calm.

"Yes, we'll tar and feather you," responded Baxter.

"And lay it on—ahem—thick, Daniel," put in Josiah Crabtree.

"Trust me for that."

Baxter gave a signal to the two tramps and they began to literally rip Tom's clothing from his back. Soon the unfortunate youth was stripped to the waist. Then Baxter caught up, a brush full of tar and advanced upon him.

CHAPTER X
IN THE NICK OF TIME

"Baxter, don't you dare to tar me!" cried Tom, as the bully faced him.

"Ha! ha! I guess you are pretty well scared now," laughed Baxter. "Your former show of bravery was all put on."

"If you go ahead you shall suffer the full penalty for the outrage, mark my words."

"Bah, Tom Rover, you can't frighten me. When I get through with you I'll warrant that your own mother won't know you."

Tom tried to retreat, but each of the tramps held him by the arm, so that he could not stir. As his legs were still bound, kicking was likewise out of the question.

"Let me put a nice big cross on his breast first," said Baxter. "Here goes!"

He reached out with the brush, but before he could touch Tom an interruption came as forceful as it was unexpected.

A thick stick came flying through the air, hitting his arm and sending the tar brush spinning to a distance.

"You rascal, let Tom alone!" came in Dick Rover's voice, and he rushed in and threw the bully headlong.

"Dick! Sam!" came from Tom joyfully. "Oh, how glad I am that you have come."

"Wot's dis!" gasped Stumpy Nuggs. "Longback, dare's trouble ahead!"

"Yes, an' I don't intend ter be in it!" answered the second tramp. "I reckon we've got about all we want out of dis crowd, anyway!" And both tramps took to their heels.

Josiah Crabtree stood by, speechless. The interruption had come so suddenly that he knew not what to do.

As quickly as he could Dan Baxter scrambled to his feet. As he did so Sam leaped for the tar brush and secured it.

"Let me alone!" roared the bully, and began to back away. But as he did so his hand went into his hip pocket and he drew a pistol.

"No, you don't!" cried Sam, and knocked the weapon from his hand with the brush. This action caused the hot tar to leave a heavy streak over Baxter's face and neck, and he let out a yell that would have done credit to an Indian on the warpath.

"Wait, I'll get even for this, Sam Rover!" he hissed, and then as Dick advanced he turned and took to his heels, running as if the Evil One were after him. Sam followed him, still swinging the brush, but Dan Baxter was soon lost to sight in the bushes.

Dick now turned to where Josiah Crabtree had been standing. The former teacher had recovered and was making tracks down the gully toward the lake. The tramps had disappeared. He leaped to Tom's side.

"We must bag some of them, Tom," he said, as he whipped out his knife and set his brother free.

"There goes Crabtree—let us collar him."

Both boys ran as never before, and came upon the former teacher just as that individual reached the lake shore below the bluff. Tom made a grab and caught him by the coat tails.

"Let me go!" snarled Crabtree, and aimed a blow at the cadet's head. But Tom ducked, and the next instant put out his foot and Crabtree pitched headlong into the lake.

"Help me! I'll be drowned!" spluttered the former teacher, as he came up with his head covered with mud, for the lake at this point was less than five feet deep.

"Climb out and you'll be all right," sang out Dick, and feeling the bottom with his feet, Crabtree looked very sheepish and clambered slowly up the bank.

As he stood before them, all dripping with water and mud, he looked the picture of misery.

"Boys, this is a—a—sad way in which to treat your former teacher," he wailed.

"Don't talk like that, or I'll be tempted to throw you in again," exclaimed Tom. "Dick, what will we do with him?"

"Hold him until we hear from Sam."

They looked up the gully and soon espied the youngest Rover hurrying toward them.

"Where is Baxter?" asked Dick.

"He got away, but not until I had let him have that tar brush right in the neck," answered Sam. "Hullo, so you have captured old Crabby, eh? That's good."

"Surely you do not intend to—ahem—keep me a prisoner," remarked Josiah Crabtree, in a voice which he tried in vain to steady.

"That's just what we do intend to do," answered Dick. "You'll march right to the Cedarville lock-up with us."

While Dick and Sam guarded the prisoner, Tom ran back for his torn coat and other garments, and also for the rope. When he returned Crabtree's hands were bound and the cadets told him to move along. He was searched, and a pistol was taken from him.

Crabtree went along most unwillingly. Once he refused to budge, but Dick showed the pistol, and that settled his stubbornness, and he went along as willingly as a lamb.

On the outskirts of Cedarville the party met Chief Burger and Detective Trigger.

"So you have one of them, eh?" cried the chief. "Very good, very good indeed. Turn him over to me and I will take him straight to headquarters."

"You must be careful that he doesn't get away," said Dick.

"Just so, lad; I will be. No one ever escaped from me, not much! Come on, sir!" And he caught Josiah Crabtree by the arm.

"This is awful!" groaned the former teacher. "And right here in Cedarville, too, where everybody knows me!"

"You should have thought of those things before, Mr. Crabtree," said Dick, his heart softening a little, now that he saw the man was beginning to break down.

"What will my friends, and the profession at large, say?" and Crabtree shook his head bitterly.

"You have only yourself to blame," put in Tom. He had not forgotten how Crabtree had threatened him but a short while before.

Suddenly the former teacher's last drop of courage seemed to desert him and, deadly pale, he sank on his knees.

"Spare me, boys, spare me! For the sake of my family and my friends, spare me!" he moaned.

"I didn't know you had a family," put in Sam.

"My relatives—my poor, dear, distant relatives," replied Crabtree, hardly aware of what he was saying. "Spare me for their sakes, and I will reward you well."

"The law must take its course, Mr. Crabtree," said Dick. He turned to Chief Burger. "Take him, and Tom can go with you, to make the charge for us and for Mrs. Stanhope. I think Detective Trigger had better come with Sam and me to hunt for Dan Baxter."

So it was arranged, and soon Crabtree was walking into Cedarville with the chief of police on one side of him and Tom on the other. The sight of a man being placed under arrest was an unusual one, and soon a crowd began to follow the three.

"It's Mr. Crabtree that used to teach at Putnam Hall," said one. "My, but ain't he a sight."

"Must have tried to get away by jumping into the lake," suggested another.

"What's he arrested for?" asked a third.

Nobody in the crowd knew, and consequently all followed to the police headquarters.

Here Chief Burger, who also acted as justice of police, took down Tom's charge against the former teacher.

"Breaking in and trying to steal," said Tom.

"It's not so!" cried Crabtree. "Boy, this is—ahem—infamous! I never stole a thing in my life!"

"We will prove it when your trial comes off," answered Tom coolly.

"Let us—ahem—try to patch this thing up," went on Josiah Crabtree. "Chief, will you kindly send for Mrs. Stanhope? I am certain she will not allow this charge to stand against me."

"See here, you shan't try any of your games on that lady!" exclaimed Tom. "I know the peculiar influence you exert over her, and I feel bound to protect her."

"She is not my enemy, as you are. I know she will clear me."

"Not much. If she won't testify against you, her daughter Dora will, and so will I and my brothers, and some other folks, too."

"I demand to see my accusers!" stormed Crabtree, trying to put on a bold front.

"All right, Dick and Sam will be here after awhile. And then, if you wish, we'll air all of your doings since the time Captain Putnam discharged you."

At the last words the former teacher winced and turned pale, for he knew his record would not bear investigating.

"You are a bad boy, Tom Rover—leave me!" he muttered, and turned his back on the cadet. A few minutes later, as he could not furnish bail, he was led to a cell and locked up.

As soon as Crabtree was disposed of, Tom left the jail to find his brothers. This was no easy matter, and it was not until well along in the afternoon that he discovered Dick, Sam, and Detective Trigger down by the lake shore nearly a mile from Cedarville.

"Any luck?" he asked.

"Not a bit," replied Dick. "He has given us the slip nicely."

The hunt continued until nightfall, and was kept up all of the next day. But it proved of no avail. Dan Baxter had left the vicinity of the lake entirely, and the Rover boys were destined not to see him again for many days to come.

The arrest of Josiah Crabtree had occurred on Friday. On Monday came a letter from Mr. Anderson Rover, stating that Alexander Pop would arrive in Cedarville on Tuesday and might remain at Mrs. Stanhope's cottage as long as the lady and the boys wished.

"I wish Aleck to be near you," wrote Mr. Rover. "It alarms me greatly to hear of the trouble that you are having. It seems to me that our family are bound to be in hot water all the time. I cannot understand Arnold Baxter. As he is in prison at Albany I do not see how he can trouble me, at least for the next few years.

"I have looked up that mining property in Colorado very carefully, and shall go out there as soon as the coming winter is at an end. Perhaps I will take one or all of you with me, but that will depend upon how good you do at your studies this winter. I shan't take anybody along that can't show a good report."

CHAPTER XI
BROUGHT TO TRIAL

"By jinks! we'll have to be on our good behavior," observed Tom, after he had read his father's letter.

"That's so," responded Sam. "Father means to have us study, or else we must stay here during the spring term."

As anticipated, Alexander Pop reached Cedarville Tuesday afternoon.

He came first to Putnam Hall, and was warmly received both by the Rover boys and by the others who knew him as an old hand around the

Hall.

"Glad you have come, Aleck!" cried Tom. "I declare it looks as if you belonged here."

"Yes, sah, an' I dun feel like I belong heah, too, Massah Tom," answered the colored man.

"Remember the sport we used to have?" put in Sam.

"'Deed I does, Massah Sam—an' de tricks youse lads used to play on dis yeah coon," and Aleck smiled broadly.

Captain Putnam also came forward to greet Pop. There had been a time when the captain had suspected Pop of stealing, and the colored man had run away in preference to being sent to jail, but now it was known by all that the faithful negro was innocent, and the master, of the Hall was sorry that he had ever accused the man.

"Pop, I miss you a good deal," he said kindly.

"If ever you are out of work again, come to me and I will let you stay here as long as you please."

"T'ank you, Cap'n Putnam, I'll remember dat. But I dun lub de Robers, ain't no use ter talk, an' so long as da wants me to stay by 'em, why dat's whar you will find Aleck Pop, yes, sah!" And he bobbed his head to emphasize his words.

"I do not blame you for sticking by them," answered the captain. "For they always stood up for you."

Of course some of the boys could not help but have some fun with Pop. Some ran off with his hat, and when they returned it to him it was half full of flour, although he did not know it.

"Mustn't do dat, Larry Colby," he said, as he took the hat. "Dis niggah dun cotch cole in his haid widout a hat." And then they clapped the headgear on his head, very carefully.

"Only a bit of Larry's sport," said Frank. "Come in, the captain wants to give you some supper before you start out for the Stanhopes' place."

Never suspecting that anything was wrong, Aleck Pop entered the kitchen attached to the academy, where Mrs. Green, the matron, had a nice supper spread for him.

"How do you do, Aleck," she said pleasantly, as he came in.

"How do yo' do, Missus Green," he answered, and took his hat off with such a flourish that part of the flour swept into her face and the balance landed over the supper table.

"Oh! oh!" screamed Mrs. Green. "What in the world have you done? I am covered with flour from head to foot!" And then she began to sneeze with great violence.

"Deed, missus, I don't—ker—chew!" replied Pop, sneezing. "I didn't—ker—chew—"

"But you did—ker—chew!" she answered. "You covered me with—ker—chew! Ker—chew!"

"Oh, you—ker—chew!" and then she went off into another prolonged sneeze.

Pop had gotten some of the flour in his eyes, indeed, his face was white from top to bottom, and it was several minutes before he could see what he was doing. His sneezing made him bump his head against the kitchen shelf, and at a point where sat a bowl of rice pudding. Part of the pudding was plastered to his forehead, while the balance turned over on to the cat sleeping on the floor.

"Me-ow!" wailed the cat, and started across the kitchen on a run, nearly upsetting Mrs. Green in its hurry to get away from more trouble.

"Stop! Did you kick my pet cat?" screamed Mrs. Green. "Oh, you—ker—chew! You brute! I never—ker—chew! Ker—chew!" And then she had to stop talking and let the sneezing have full play.

"I didn't kick—ker—chew—nuffin!" spluttered Aleck. "I'se dun—ker—chew—dem boys dun—ker—chew! Dern boys did it."

"Did what?"

"Put flour in ma hat, de ole boy take 'em!" finished Aleck, and then he blundered out of the kitchen and tried to find Larry and the others. But all of the cadets, who had been watching proceedings through the kitchen window, had vanished and could not be found.

A couple of hours later Tom and Dick took the colored man down to the Stanhope cottage. Mrs. Stanhope already knew the man well, as did Dora, and both were glad that he had come to stay with them. Pop had brought along a pistol, and also a war club he had picked up in Africa, and declared himself ready to meet any and all comers.

"I'se dun learned how to shoot putty straight," he remarked. "So de fellers wot prowls around bettah look out fo' demselbes."

"Crabtree is in jail, so you will only have Dan Baxter to guard against," said Dick. "And I hardly think he will show up in a hurry."

That night Dick and Tom had a long conversation with Mrs. Stanhope. The lady was very nervous, and when asked if she would appear against Josiah Crabtree she shivered from head to foot.

"I—I cannot do it," she said brokenly. "Do not ask it of me! He—he— I cannot face him without he makes me feel as if I were in his power."

"He is something of a hypnotist," said Tom. "Cannot you remember that, and nerve yourself against coming under his spell?"

But the lady only shivered again. "No! no! I have tried it—for Dora's sake—but I cannot do it! I am horrified at his influence, but I cannot withstand it."

"Then you will keep away from the court room when he is tried?"

"Yes, I must. I will get my doctor to issue a certificate that I am ill."

"Will you let Dora testify? If she wishes to do so."

There the matter rested, and the two boys sought out Dora.

"It is too bad," said Dick, on the way. "Mrs. Stanhope is on the verge of a nervous collapse, and I believe it is all on account of Crabtree's doings."

"Yes, and I am afraid she will never get away from his influence. If he hadn't been something of a hypnotist I don't believe she would ever have taken to him at the start as she did."

When Dora was told of what her mother had said, she felt like crying, and the tears stood in her eyes.

"I know it all only too well," she said. "I am glad mamma mill not face him. Why, he would influence her into declaring that he was innocent!"

"But you will testify, won't you?" asked Dick earnestly.

"If you wish it, Dick. But I hate the publicity."

"Crabtree ought to be put where he can do your mother no further harm."

"Yes, I feel that, too."

"And you must remember how he helped to abduct you."

"I haven't forgot that."

Vick and Tom remained until it was quite late, and then almost ran back to the Hall, for the captain had told them not to be out after eleven o'clock.

For several days matters ran smoothly at the Hall. Then came Josiah Crabtree's trial, and all of the Rover boys went to the county seat, to remain several days. With them went Dora and her uncle, John Laning.

The former teacher's trial lasted longer than expected, and the jury were out the best part of a night before arriving at a verdict. In the end, much to the Rover boys' surprise, Crabtree was sentenced to six months in the county jail, instead of to several years in the State's prison.

"I can't understand it," muttered Dick, when, they were on the way back to the Hall. "He must have hypnotized the judge who tried the case." The verdict was a disappointing one, yet it was something to know that Crabtree would be out of the way even that long.

"Before he gets out you can be on your trip to Buffalo and the Great Lakes," said Dick to Dora. "And perhaps you can hide your whereabouts from him, so that he can't get at your mother, to try on his game again."

"I will certainly try to throw him off the track," answered the girl. "I never want to see him again."

Captain Putnam was anxious to learn how the trial had ended, and came from the academy on horseback to meet the boys.

"Well, it is something," he said, half-smiling. "But you are right, he deserved more."

"I knew he was no good," said Tom. "Knew it from the first time I met him, when he was head assistant here, and placed me under arrest for shooting off a fire-cracker at the gate."

At this Captain Putnam laughed outright.

"You have a good memory, Thomas, I must say! Well, you are square now, as you boys call it."

CHAPTER XII
WINTER DAYS AT PUTNAM HALL

After the trial of Josiah Crabtree the days flew by swiftly at the Hall. Bound to make a good showing, each of the Rover boys applied himself diligently to his studies, and all made rapid progress.

Thanksgiving came and went, and a week later there came a fairly heavy fall of snow.

"Hurrah! winter is knocking at the door at last!" cried Sam joyfully. "Now for some snowballing, skating, and all the rest of the winter fun."

Snowballing was already going on, and the white balls were flying in all directions. Dick had his hat taken off by Frank, and in return filled Frank's ear with snow. Tom and Fred got into a regular war at close quarters, and in the end Tom threw his opponent flat and stuffed snow down his neck. But then Larry came up with a huge cake of snow and nearly smothered Tom, and then a dozen leaped in, and a good-natured melee resulted, lasting for the rest of the playtime.

It was very cold that night, and two days later the ice on the lake was two inches thick. Still the captain made the boys wait until the following Saturday, when the ice was strong enough to bear a horse.

In the meantime skates had been brought out and polished up, and soon the edge of the lake was alive with skaters, all moving swiftly from one spot to another, and shrieking and laughing at the top of their voices. George Strong, the assistant master, also came down and showed some of the older boys how to cut fancy figures. Dick was a good skater, and took to the fancy figures with ease. As for Tom and Sam, they preferred straight skating, and entered half a dozen trials of speed down the lake to the old boathouse and back.

"If it gets much colder, so that the ice thickens, I am going to build an ice-boat," said Frank to Dick that night. "Captain Putnam said I could have all the old lumber I want. You know the carpenters left a lot when they fixed over that burnt part of the Hall."

"Hurrah, an ice-boat!" cried Dick. "Just the thing. Let me help, you, Frank. Perhaps the captain will let us have an old camping-out tent for a sail."

"Yes, I've asked him about that already, and he told Mrs. Green to get me one from the storehouse."

"And what about nails and runners?"

"Peleg Snuggers is going to give me the nails and lend me the tools. The runners I will have to buy down to the blacksmith shop."

"There is an old cask down at the boathouse. We can take the hoops from that and have the blacksmith straighten them out, and they will do first rate for runners."

So the talk ran on, and on the following Monday, as the cold continued, the boys set to work, during the off-time, to build the ice-boat. Tom, Sam, and Hans joined in, and as soon as the frame was put together the boat was christened the Fiver, because, as Frank declared, it was built to hold just five and no more.

There was a class devoted to manual training at the Hall, so all of the boys were acquainted with the use of tools. The building of the iceboat progressed rapidly, and soon all that were wanting were the sail and the runners. Frank and Dick procured the hoops and had the blacksmith straighten them out and punch holes into them, and Mrs. Green kindly transformed an old tent into a mainsail of no mean proportions. As a matter of fact it would have been better for the boys had the sail been smaller.

It was a rather cloudy Saturday half-holiday when the boys placed the ice-boat on rollers and rolled it down to the lake front. All of the other cadets watched the proceedings with interest, and were sorry they could not go on the proposed trip. But Frank promised that all should have their turns later on.

A fair breeze was blowing, and no sooner was the mainsail raised than the Fiver, moved off in such a lively fashion that Tom, who had lingered behind, had all he could do to run and get on board.

"We're off! Hurrah!" yelled Sam, and the others took up the cry, and both those on board and those left behind waved hats and caps in the air and set up a cheer.

"And now where shall we go?" asked Frank, as they whizzed along.

"That will depend upon the wind," came from Tom. "Remember, we must get back before seven o'clock."

"Yah, der vint is eferydings," put in Hans. "Supposin' ve git far avay und der vint sthops plowing, vot den?"

"Then we'll set you on the rear seat to blow the sail yourself," replied Frank. "This wind is good for all day, and I know it," he added emphatically.

"Let us follow the shore for the present," said Tom. "Perhaps the Pornell students are skating below here and we can show them what we are up to."

So on they went along the shore, until the wind began to change and carry them out into the lake. Here the ice was, however, far from safe, and they began to tack back.

"It's snowing!" cried Sam presently. He was right, and ere long the flakes were coming down thickly. With the coming of the snow the wind died out utterly.

"Here's a pickle," muttered Tom, in disgust. "Frank, I thought you said this wind was good for all day?"

"Frank must haf had his schleepin' cap on ven he said dot," put in Hans, and the others set up a laugh.

"Well, I did think the wind would hold out," replied Frank, with a wry face. "This is going to spoil everything. Did anybody bring his skates?"

Nobody had, although all had calculated to do so. In the excitement every pair had been forgotten.

"Now we can't even skate home," said Dick.

"And I rather think it will be a long walk — at least three miles."

"That's not the worst of it," came from his youngest brother. "Look how heavily it is snowing."

"Poch! who's afraid of a little snow?" blustered Tom.

"Nobody, but if we can't see our way—"

"By Jove! I never thought of that!" groaned Frank. "Just look around, boys. It's awful, isn't it?"

Much startled, all looked around. On every hand the snow was coming down so thickly that they could not see a distance of two rods in any direction.

"We seem to be cut off," observed Dick soberly. "I reckon the best thing we can do is to make for shore."

"And leave the Fiver behind?"

"No. Let us lower the sail and push her in front of us."

This was considered good advice, and much put out over the sudden termination of their sport, the five cadets lowered the sail and tied it up, and then leaped to the ice.

"Now then, all together!" cried Frank, but to his surprise Tom and Hans pushed in a different direction to the others.

"Why, Tom, that's not the way!" cried Frank.

"Isn't it?" burst out Tom. "Why not?"

"Because it isn't."

"Of course dot is der vay," cried Hans. "Der shore vos ofer dare."

"Yes, the other shore. But not the one we left and the one we want to get back to."

A long discussion followed, and it was soon realized that either Tom and Hans, or else the others, were sadly mixed up. "The majority rules," said Frank. "So let us go this way."

"All right, I will," grumbled Tom. "But I still think you are wrong."

"And I vos sure of him," added Hans.

However, they took hold willingly enough, and soon the whole party were moving slowly through the snowstorm, shoving the Fiver in front of them. The snow had now become blinding, and absolutely nothing was to be seen around them.

A half hour had passed, and they were wondering why the shore did not appear, when suddenly Dick uttered a warning cry.

"Look out! We are going into the open water! Back all of you!"

They leaped back, fairly tumbling over each other in their efforts to escape the water, which crept up to their feet without warning. As they pushed themselves back they naturally sent the Fiver flying forward, and an instant later they heard a crashing of ice and saw the ice-boat topple over into the water and disappear from view!

CHAPTER XIII
LOST IN THE SNOW

"The ice-boat's gone!"

"Get back, boys, or we'll all be in the water!"

Ca-a-ac-ck! A long warning sound rang through the snow-laden air and the party of five felt the surface of the ice parting beneath them. They turned and sped away from the water with all the speed at their command, and soon the dangerous spot was left behind, but not before poor Hans had lost his cap and Sam had gotten his left foot wet to the ankle.

"By jinks! but that was a narrow shave!" gasped Dick, when they were safe. "A little more and all of us would have been under the ice."

"And that would have cost us our lives!" said Frank solemnly. "Boys, I don't believe I'll ever want to go ice-boating again."

"Mine cap vos gone," growled the German cadet dismally. "How vos I going to keep mine head from freezing, tole me dot, vill you?"

"That's rough on you," said Tom. "Here, take my tippet and tie that around your head and ears." And he took the article in question and handed it over.

"Dank you, Tom, you vos a goot feller. But vot you vos do to keep your neck varm, hey?"

"Here's a silk handkerchief, he can wear that," said Dick. "But I say, fellows," he went on. "I think we are mixed up now and no mistake."

"I am sure I am," answered Frank. "I haven't the least idea where the shore is."

"Nor I," came from Tom. "We'll have to go at it in a hit-or-miss fashion."

"No miss for me," put in Sam. "I am not prepared for a watery grave just now."

"We must be cautious," said Dick. "I've got an idea. Has anybody a rope with him?"

"I've got a heavy cord," answered Frank.

"Then let us tie that to each fellow's right wrist. Then we can string out in a line, like the Swiss mountain climbers, and if the boy in front gets into trouble the others can haul him out."

"Hurrah! Dick, has solved the problem of how the lost cadets are going to get to safety," cried Sam. "Let us have the cord by all means."

It was quickly produced and proved to be about forty feet in length. Dick tied himself fast to one end and Sam the other, and the others came between.

"Now then, forward march!" shouted Dick. And on they moved, in Indian file.

"Route step!" shouted Frank. And they broke up as ordered — that is each walking to suit himself, so that their feet should not come down on the ice at the same time, something which might have cause another cracking.

The snow still came down as hard as ever — indeed, to Dick it appeared to come down harder. The wind was beginning to rise again and blew the blinding particles directly into their faces.

"What's the use of walking right in the teeth of the wind," grumbled Tom. "Why not try the other way?"

"I think the wind comes from off shore, that's why," answered his elder brother.

"I don't. I think it's coming down the lake."

"I believe Dick is right," ventured Frank. "The wind came that way before — that is why we were blown out so far."

The matter was put to a vote and all but Tom agreed that they must be heading for the western shore of the lake. So the weary tramp was resumed.

It was not without its incidents. Once Hans' feet went from under him and he went flat on his back, taking Tom with him. This caused the line to tighten and all went on top of the pair and a grand melee resulted. Then Tom playfully filled Sam's neck with snow, and Hans let a little snowball drop into Tom's ear, and in a second all were at it in a snow fight which lasted several minutes.

At last Dick arose and shook himself. "Hi! this won't do!" he cried, brushing himself off. "Unless we hurry we'll be late in getting back."

"Late in getting back?" repeated Frank. "I shall count myself lucky if we don't have remain here all night."

"Great Caesar, Frank, do you mean that?" came from Sam.

"I do. Here we have been tramping I don't know how long, and we seem to be as far from shore as ever."

"Exactly so," grumbled Hans. "I dink ve must pe moving around in a ring, hey?"

"Can that be possible?" asked Tom.

"I don't think so," answered Dick, "for I have been watching the ice very closely and I haven't seen the first sign of our doubling our steps."

"Let us keep out in a straight line," said Tom. "That will keep us away from the circle business."

Once more they pushed on, but the snow was now several inches deep, and the ice very slippery and all of the party could scarcely drag one foot after the other. It was Sam who called another halt.

"I'm getting winded!" he panted. "Boys, I guess we are lost in the snow."

"That's true, Sam," said Frank. "The shore seems to be as far off as ever."

"I told you that you were wrong," put in Tom. "If we had been walking toward shore we would be on land long ago."

"I don't know but what Tom's view is correct," said Frank slowly,

"Unless we've been moving in a crooked line, as Hans suggested," said the elder Rover.

One and another of the little party gazed at his companions and then at the desolate scene around them. Yes, they were lost in the snowstorm, and what the end of the adventure would be they could not imagine.

"Well, we can try Tom's course," said Dick, after another careful look around which is not saving much as the snow was coming down as thickly as ever.

"I notice that it is getting dark," observed Frank, as they trudged on. "I wonder what time it is?"

A watch was consulted and they learned to their chagrin that it was half-past four.

"I vos gitting hungry," came from Hans.

"Don't say a word!" cried Tom. "I could eat a doughnut a month old."

"Don't speak about it," put in Dick dryly. "It will only make you feel more hungry."

Darkness was coming on rapidly, and all of the boys were beginning to despair when suddenly Dick gave a shout of joy.

"The shore, boys! The shore at last!"

"Where?" came from all of the others.

"Over to our left. Come on!"

The others followed Dick willingly and in less than half a minute found themselves on solid earth once more, but at some point where the ground was little more than a stretch of flat meadow land.

"Hurrah!" shouted Sam. "How good to be on land once more!"

"Perhaps we might have been on land long ago if we had turned to the left," observed Frank. "We may have been skirting the shore for half the afternoon!"

"Never mind, we are here at last so don't let's grumble," said Tom. "What's that ahead, a barn?"

"Some kind of a building," answered Dick. "Let us go forward and investigate."

They did so, and found a half tumbled down building, which had once been used for the storage of meadow hay and also as a boathouse. The door was gone and the window broken out, and the snow lay on the floor to the depth of an inch or more.

But still it was more pleasant inside than out, for the wind was rising and the large flakes of snow had given place to fine hard particles which came swishing down like so much sharp salt, so Dick said. It cut into their faces and made them thankful that some shelter had been found, no matter how humble.

It was too dark now to see anything, and sitting on some old hay in the most sheltered corner of the building the five boys held a consultation.

"I move we stay here until morning," said Tom. "If we go out again we may be lost and frozen to death."

"That is true," commented Frank. "But what will Captain Putnam say?"

"He can't blame us for what has happened," said Dick. "We tried our best to get back."

"Yah, und he vos know ve ton't stay here nildowit suppers for noddings," was the manner in which the German cadet expressed himself.

"Oh, Hans, how can you!" broke from Tom, who could eat at any time, and who now felt more hungry than any of them. "Do you mean to say we'll have to remain here all night without our suppers!"

"Vell, vot else you vos going ter do, hey?"

"We'll have to go without something to eat, unless we can find something close at hand," said Frank.

One after another went out to the doorway and to the open window and gazed forth. But the howling wind and blinding snow soon made all glad enough to get back to the sheltered corner. It was now pitch dark.

"We are in for it, so make yourselves as comfortable as possible," observed Frank. "My, how the wind does blow!"

"It's like a hurricane in an African forest," said Sam. "I believe it's almost strong enough to take a fellow off his feet."

The wind kept increasing in violence, until the old barn seemed to rock back and forth. It arose in a low moan and mounted steadily to a shriek, gradually dying away in the distance, followed by the slish-slishing of the fine snow across the rotted shingles of the roof.

"It's a tempest not to be forgotten," said Frank. "I can't remember when I've heard the wind make such a noise before. If it gets any worse it—"

Frank got no further, for the shrieking of the wind drowned out every other sound. Then came a strange grinding and creaking overhead, and the barn rocked more than ever.

"Get out, boys," yelled Tom. "The old shebang is going to pieces!"

Tom had scarcely spoken when the shock came, and beams, boards, and shingles flew in all directions. It was a terrifying occurrence and not knowing what else to do the five boys dug into the loose hay and threw themselves flat. Each felt as if the end of the world had come.

CHAPTER XIV
A FEW SPRING HAPPENINGS

Luckily for the boys the barn was blown clean over on its side, its roof falling some distance away, so that none of the wreckage came down on top of the crowd.

But the sounds of the beams and boards breaking were so terrifying that for several minutes after the damage was done none of the crowd dared to move. Each felt as though the next second might be his last.

At length Dick pulled himself together and peered forth.

"Any—anybody hurt?" he panted.

"I'm not," came from Tom. "But, say, wasn't—"

A splutter, coming from Hans, interrupted him. In his eagerness to escape the fall of the barn the German cadet had plunged into the hay open-mouthed, and now some of the stuff had entered his throat and was almost choking him.

"Clap him on the back!" cried Dick, and Tom did as requested. Then came several gulps and Hans began to cough. But the danger from strangulation was over.

All were soon out of the wreckage, and thankful that they had escaped thus easily.

"But we won't have the barn to shelter us," said Frank ruefully. "What will we do next?"

"Push on until another shelter appears," said Dick. "We can't remain here, to be frozen to death."

"Yes, but be careful that we don't get on to the lake again," cautioned Sam.

"No fear of that, Sam."

After the terrific blow which laid low the old barn, the wind appeared to let up a bit, and consequently moving was not so difficult. They struck out across the meadow, and presently gained a clump of trees.

"Dis vos besser as noddings," said Hans. "Supposing ve stay here for der night?"

"I'm going to see what's on the other side of the woods first," replied Dick, and stalked off, Tom at his heels. Presently the others heard both Rover boys set up a shout.

"A house, fellows! Come on!"

They made a rush forward, and soon they reached a stone fence. On the other side was what had been a planted field, and beyond this a house and several outbuildings.

With hearts greatly lightened they climbed over the fence and made for the house. They were still some distance from the dwelling when they heard the bark of a dog.

"Hullo! I hope he isn't loose," cried Frank.

"But he is," ejaculated Tom; "and he is coming this way too!"

"Du meine zeit!" shrieked Hans. "He vill chew us all up! Vot shall ve do?" And he looked ready to collapse.

"Perhaps we can snowball him—" began Sam, when Dick set up another cry.

"It's Laning's dog, boys. What fools we are! This is Mr. Laning's place."

"Laning's place," burst out Tom. "Why, to be sure it is. And that is Leo! Leo! Leo! old boy, don't you know us?" he cried.

On bounded the dog, and then began to bark again, but this time joyously. He came up to Tom and leaped all around him, wagging his brush as he did so. Then he came to Sam and to Dick, for he knew them all very well.

"It's a good thing the old barn blew down," said Tom, for he could not help but think of the greeting the Laning girls would give him.

They were soon at the back door of the farmer's cottage. It was opened by Mrs. Laning, who stared at them in astonishment.

"Can we come in?" asked Dick. "We are nearly frozen."

"Well, I never! Out in all this storm! It's a wonder the captain would allow it. Why, come in of course, and get thawed out by the fire." And then they went in to meet Mr. Laning, and also the two girls.

Their story was soon told, and meanwhile the lady of the house prepared a hot supper for them. As they sat eating they discussed the question of whether it would be better to return to Putnam Hall that night or wait until morning.

"I would say stay here," said Mr. Laning, "but Captain Putnam will be worried about you and start out in search of you."

"That's just it," answered Dick. "I think one of us, at least, ought to return."

"Let us draw straws for it," said Frank, and so it was agreed.

From the Laning place each knew the road well, so there was no danger of going astray. Besides, the storm was now letting up in violence.

It fell to Frank's choice to go, and as he was about to leave Hans decided to keep him company. The pair was soon off, and this left the Rover boys and the Lanings to themselves.

Satisfied that all was now right, the three brothers made the most of the evening thus afforded them, and so did the two girls, and all played, sang, and went in for various games until eleven o'clock. Then the lads retired to a room assigned to them.

"I say," said Tom, as he prepared to turn in. "That adventure started queer-like, but we came out of it all right."

"Yes, it couldn't be better," added Sam.

At this Dick winked. "Especially as we landed at the Lanings' home," he observed.

"What a pity it wasn't Dora's home, too," drawled Tom, and then as Dick shied a shoe at him he turned over and dropped off into the land of dreams.

Early the next morning they started for Putnam Hall, John Laning driving them thither in his sleigh. It was a ride they enjoyed. The farmer dropped them at the door, and Captain Putnam stood ready to receive them.

"I am glad you are safe back," he said, with some display of emotion. "Harrington and Mueller have given me the particulars of your night's adventure. Hereafter I want all of the cadets to remain off the lake during a snowstorm."

"You may be sure we will remain off, captain," answered Dick. "One such adventure is enough for any fellow."

After this happening nothing of special interest occurred until Christmas. Then the cadets gave their usual entertainment, including a little domestic drama called "Looking for a Quiet Boarding House." In this drama Tom and Larry acted the parts of two old maids who were taking boarders, while Dick, Sam, and eight others were the so-called boarders, or those looking for board. The play was filled with humorous situations, and the audience, in which were the Stanhopes and the Lanings, enjoyed it hugely.

"If you fail in everything else, you had better go on the stage, Tom," said Nellie to that youth. "You make a splendid actor—or I should say actress," and she laughed.

"How would you like to have me for a sister?" minced Tom, in the voice he had used in acting.

"Thank you, but I don't want an old maid for a sister."

"Then perhaps you don't want to be an old maid yourself," he retorted. "All right, I'll see to it that you are spared that annoyance." And then she boxed him playfully on the ears. She could not help but think a good deal of this open-hearted, fun-loving fellow.

After the entertainment the boys went home, to remain over New Year's Day. Jack Ness, the hired man, met them at the railroad station in Oak Run and drove them through Dexter's Corners to Valley Brook farm.

"It's good fer sore eyes to see ye back," said the hired man. "The folks is waitin' fer ye like a set o' children."

When they came in sight of the farmhouse there were Mr. Rover, Uncle Randolph, and Aunt Martha all on the porch to receive them. Anderson Rover could not help rushing forward to embrace his sons, and the greetings of uncle and aunt were scarcely less affectionate.

"My own boys!" was all that Anderson Rover said, but the manner of speaking meant a good deal.

"The house is yours, boys," said their Aunt Martha. "I used to think you were a bother, but now I'd rather have the bother than miss you," and she smiled so sweetly that Dick gave her an extra hug.

"Yes, yes, do what you please, lads," put in Randolph Rover. "I shall not be annoyed. We understand each other a great deal better than we did before we went to Africa, eh?"

"Right you are, uncle!" cried Tom. "We found you out to be a regular brick."

Christmas presents were numerous, including some jewelry for all of the boys and a ring to replace the one Tom had lost, and some games, and half a dozen story books, not to mention other things more useful, as, for instance, some socks Mrs. Randolph Rover had, herself, made. For the aunt there was a new breastpin from the three boys, and for the uncle a set of scientific works just to his liking. For their father the lads had purchased a gold-headed cane, the stick of which was made of some wood they had brought with them from the banks of the Congo.

The time at home passed all too quickly, and soon it was necessary for the boys to return to Putnam Hall. Dora Stanhope and the Laning girls had not been forgotten, and now these young folks sent gifts of dainty embroidered handkerchiefs, of which the boys were very proud. Tom and Sam had sent Nellie and Grace two elegant Christmas cards. What Dick had sent Dora he would not tell. Being behind the scenes we may state that it was a tiny gold locket, heart-shaped, and that Dora treasured the gift highly.

The second week after New Year found them at the Hall once more, pegging away at their studies harder than ever, for they were bound to make the record their father desired of them.

But the time spent at school was not without its sport and fun, for there was plenty of sleighing and skating, and the gymnasium was always open during the off hours.

"No enemies at the Hall this season," remarked Fred Garrison, "no Baxters or Cavens, or fellows of that sort."

"No, and I am glad of it," answered Dick. "It's a big relief."

"Have you any idea what became of Baxter?"

"Not the slightest."

"And of Mumps, the fellow who used to be his toady?"

"Oh, Mumps reformed, after that chase on the ocean, and I've since heard that he went West, struck some sort of a job as a bookkeeper, or something like that."

"Well, old Crabtree is safe. He won't bother you any more," concluded Fred, and there the subject dropped.

The weeks glided by quickly, until spring was at hand, and the green grass began to cover the bills and fields surrounding Cayuga Lake. Still the Rover boys pegged away, and it must be admitted that even Captain Putnam was astonished at their progress.

"They are whole-souled fellows," he said to George Strong. "They put their whole mind into everything they go into."

"And those are the boys who afterward make their mark in the world," answered the head assistant. "The Rover boys are all right."

CHAPTER XV
HOW ARNOLD BAXTER ESCAPED

"Well, I never!"

It was Dick Rover who uttered the remark, as he leaped from the chair in which he had been sitting, newspaper in hand.

"Never what, Dick?" drawled Tom lazily, looking up from a kite he was mending.

"Never saw anything to equal those Baxters. What do you think? Arnold Baxter has escaped from prison."

"What!" ejaculated Tom, and on the instant the kite was forgotten, and Tom smashed it directly through the middle with his foot as he came to his brother's side.

"Yes, he has escaped, and in the slickest manner I ever heard of. I tell you, Tom, he is a prize criminal, if ever there was one."

"But how did he get out?"

"How? Why, just shook hands with his jailers, thanked them for their kindness, and then left."

"Oh, pshaw, Dick, is this a joke? Because if it is, I want to remind you that we had the first of April last week."

"It's no joke, although Baxter ought to have played his trick on the first, true enough."

"Well, what is the trick? You said he shook hands with his jailers and walked off. Of course, he couldn't do that, unless his time was up."

"But it wasn't up — not by several years."

"Then how did he do it?"

"By a trick, Tom — the neatest, cleverest, slickest ever performed in this State."

"Oh, stow your long-winded speeches, Dick," cried the younger brother half angrily. "Boil it down and serve the extract in short order."

"Very well, I will. Firstly, Arnold Baxter is in jail. Secondly, he states his friends are going to ask the governor for a pardon. Thirdly, a friend in disguise comes to the jail with the supposed pardon. Fourthly, great joy of Baxter. Fifthly, he thanks his jailers and bids them good-by, as I said before. Sixthly, after he and his friend are gone the jailers inspect the so-called pardon. Seventhly, the jailers telephone to the governor. Eighthly, the pardon is pronounced a forgery, signatures, seal, and all. Ninthly, all the powers that be are as mad as hornets, but they can do nothing, for Baxter the elder has gone and has left no trace behind him."

"Phew!" Tom emitted a long, low whistle.

"Say, but that runs like the half-dime novels I used to stuff myself with in my green days, doesn't it?"

"That's right, Tom, excepting that this is strictly true, while the half-dime novels used to be as far from the truth as a howling dog is from the moon. But seriously, I don't like this," went on the elder Rover earnestly.

"Neither do I like it."

"Baxter at liberty may mean trouble for father and for us."

"I begin to see now what Dan Baxter meant," ejaculated Tom suddenly. "I'll wager he knew all along what his father and the friend were up to."

"I wonder who the stranger was? He must have been a very skillful forger to forge the governor's signature and the other signatures too."

"He must be some old pal to Baxter. Don't you remember father said Baxter was thick with several fellows in the West before he came out here?"

"Let us write to father about this at once."

This was agreed to, and Dick began to pen the letter without delay. While he was at work Sam came in and was acquainted with the news.

"It's just like the Baxters," said the youngest Rover. "After this, I'll be prepared to expect anything of them. I'd like to know where he has gone? Perhaps out West."

"Out West?" cried Dick and Tom simultaneously.

"Certainly. Didn't he swear to get the best of us regarding that mine matter?"

"By gum!" murmured Tom. "Dick, we can't send that letter any too quick. Perhaps we had better telegraph."

"Oh, father may have the news already." Dick glanced at the newspaper again. "Hullo, I missed this," he cried.

"Missed what?" came from both of the others.

"The paper says Baxter's escape occurred several days ago. The prison' officials kept it to themselves at first, hoping the detectives would re-capture the criminal."

"And that paper was printed yesterday morning. At any rate, Baxter has had his liberty for at least five days. I must say I don't like this at all. We'll telegraph to father without delay."

Looking out of the window Dick saw Captain Putnam walking on the parade ground. He ran down to interview the master of the Hall.

"Why, yes, you can go to Cedarville at once, if you deem it important," said the captain. "Peleg Snuggers can drive you down."

"Thank you, captain," said Dick, and ran to the stables. He found the utility man at work cleaning out a stall, and soon had Snuggers hitching up. Inside of ten minutes Dick was on the way to town. As he bowled along, little did he dream of how long it would be before he should see dear old Putnam Hall again.

While passing the Stanhope cottage Dick saw Dora at work over a flower bed in the front garden.

"Just going to Cedarville on a little errand," he shouted, and waved his hand to her, and she waved in return. In the back garden was Aleck, and the negro, flourished a hoe as a salute.

The telegraph office at Cedarville was not a large place, and but few private messages were received there. As Dick drove up the operator looked at him and at Snuggers.

"Hullo, I was just going to send a message up to your place," he said to the utility man.

"All right, I'll take it," replied Snuggers. "You can pay me for the messenger service," he added with a grin.

"Whom is the message for, if I may ask?" questioned Dick quickly.

"For Richard Rover."

"That's myself. Let me have it at once."

"You are Richard Rover?" queried the operator, and looked at Snuggers, who nodded. "You came here just in time, then."

The telegraph operator brought the message forth, and Dick tore it open with a hand that trembled in spite of his efforts to control it. He felt instinctively that something was wrong.

The telegram was from Mrs. Randolph Rover, and ran as follows:

"Come home at once. Your father and uncle attacked by unknown rascal who tried to ransack house. Uncle seriously hurt.

"Martha Rover."

Dick's heart seemed to stop beating as he read the lines. "Attacked by rascal who tried to ransack the house," he murmured. "It must have been Arnold Baxter."

"No bad news, I trust, Master Dick," observed Snuggers.

"Yes, Peleg, very bad. Take this back to the Hall and give it to my brothers, and tell them I am going to Ithaca by the first boat, and there take the midnight train for home. Tell them to explain to Captain Putnam and then to follow me. Do you understand?"

"Well—I—er—I guess I do," stammered the workingman. "Be you going home, then?"

"At once." Dick turned to the operator.

"The boat for Ithaca is almost due, isn't it?"

"Yes, sir, in five minutes."

"Take me to the wharf, Peleg, and hurry up about it."

"Got to go, then?"

"I have," and Dick leaped into the carriage. Peleg Snuggers saw that the young cadet was in earnest, and made the boat landing in less than three minutes.

The Sylvan Dell, a companion boat to the Morning Star, was on time, and Dick soon found himself on board and bound for Ithaca. He was too excited to keep quiet, and began to pace the boat from stem to stern.

"What's up, my lad?" asked the captain, as he looked at the youth curiously.

"I am in a hurry to get home, sir."

"Well, I'm afraid tramping around won't hurry matters any," and Captain Miller smiled broadly.

"Do you object to my walking around?" asked Dick, somewhat sharply.

"Oh, no; go ahead. I hope you haven't heard any bad news," went on the captain kindly.

"But I have heard bad news. My father and my uncle were attacked by some man who tried to ransack the house. My uncle was seriously hurt."

"That's bad. I trust they collared the villain."

"No; I guess he got away, for the telegram I received said he was unknown."

"It's too bad. Do your folks live in the city?"

"No; at a country place called Valley Brook."

"Then I doubt if they catch the rascal who did the deed. The country offers too good a chance to escape."

"I mean to catch him if I can," said Dick earnestly, and then the captain left him once more to himself. He thought that the boy had rather a large opinion of himself, but did not know that Dick already had a first-class clew to work on.

CHAPTER XVI
SOMETHING ABOUT THE ECLIPSE MINE

"Dick! Oh, how glad I am that you have come!"

Mrs. Randolph Rover rushed out to the porch to greet the boy as he came bounding up the steps, two at a time.

"I came as soon as I received the telegram," he answered, as he embraced his aunt. "And how are father and Uncle Randolph?"

"Your father is not seriously hurt, — only a twist of his left ankle, where the burglar kicked him. But your Uncle Randolph — "

Mrs. Rover stopped and shook her head bitterly.

"Not dangerously hurt, I hope," cried Dick, his heart leaping into his mouth, for as we already know, his eccentric old uncle was very dear to him.

"Yes, he is seriously hurt, Dick. He was struck in the head, and a fever has set in."

"Can I see him?"

"Not yet. The doctor says he must be kept very quiet."

"But he will recover, aunt?"

"I—I hope so, Dick. Oh, it was dreadful!" And the tears rolled down the woman's pale face.

"I'm so sorry for you!" he exclaimed, brushing the tears away with his handkerchief. "So sorry. Where is father?"

"Up in the bedroom in the wing of the house."

"I can see him, can't I?"

"Oh, yes."

Dick waited to hear no more, but ran up the stairs quickly, yet making no noise, for fear of disturbing his uncle, who was in a front room on the same floor.

"Father, can I come in?" he asked in a low voice.

"Yes, Dick," was the reply, and he went into the room, to find his father in a rocking chair, with his left foot resting on a stool. Mr. Anderson Rover's face showed plainly that he had suffered considerable pain.

"Father, I am so glad it is no worse," he said, as he took his parent's hand. "Aunt Martha tells me Uncle Randolph is seriously hurt."

"Yes, he got the worst of it," returned Anderson Rover. "The blow was meant for me, but your uncle leaped in and caught its full force."

"And do you know who the robber was?"

"No; he had his face well covered."

"I think I can tell you."

"You, Dick? Ah, you are thinking of that Dan Baxter. It was a man, not a boy; I am sure of that much."

"Yes, it was a man, father. It was Arnold Baxter."

"Arnold Baxter! You must be dreaming. He is in jail."

"No, he has escaped; he escaped about a week ago."

"Escaped?" Anderson Rover raised himself up, and would have leaped to his feet hid not his sprained ankle prevented him. "You are certain of this?"

"Yes," and Dick related the particulars.

"You must be right. The man did look like Baxter, but I thought it impossible that it could be the same." The elder Rover gave a groan. "Then the fat is in the fire for a certainty. And after all my work and trouble!"

"What are you talking about now, father?"

"That mining claim in Colorado—the Eclipse Mine, as Roderick Kennedy christened it."

"But I don't understand?"

"It's a long story, Dick. You have beard parts of it, but not the whole, and to go into the details would do you small good."

"But I would like to know something, father."

"You shall know something, Dick." Mr. Rover drew up his injured foot. "Oh, if only I could go after Arnold Baxter without delay!"

"It's too bad you are hurt. Does it pain you very much?"

"When I try to stand on it the pain is terrible. The doctor says I must not use the foot for a month or six weeks."

"That will make tedious waiting for you."

"Yes, and in the meantime Baxter will try to cheat me out of that mining property, if he can."

"But he won't dare to show himself."

"He will do the work through some other party—probably the man who helped him to escape from prison."

"Did he get anything of value—papers, for instance?"

"Yes, he got most of the papers, although I still retain one small map, a duplicate of one which was stolen. You see, Dick, years ago Roderick Kennedy and myself were partners out in Colorado, owning half a dozen claims."

"Yes; I've heard that before."

"Well, one day Kennedy went off prospecting and located a very rich find, which he christened the Eclipse Mine. The claim was never worked, but he made a map of the locality, which he kept a secret. As his partner I was entitled to half of all of his discoveries, just as he was entitled to half of my discoveries.

"At that time Arnold Baxter worked for both of us. He was thick with Kennedy, and I soon saw that he was trying to break up the partnership, so that he could form a new deal with Kennedy. But Kennedy was true to me, and in the end we caught Baxter stealing from us, and gave him twenty-four hours' notice to quit camp.

"Baxter was enraged at this, and went off vowing to get square. About a month after that happened Kennedy tumbled off a cliff, and died of his injuries. In his will he left me all of his mining properties, including the Eclipse claim, which I have never yet seen.

"After Kennedy was buried Arnold Baxter came forward and claimed part of the property, and produced papers to substantiate his claims. But the papers were proved by a dozen miners to be of no value, and in the end he was again drummed out of camp.

"I was making money fast just then, and for the time being paid no attention to Baxter. But he continued to annoy me, and I am pretty certain that on one or two occasions be tried to take my life. But at last he disappeared, and I heard no more of him until you boys brought me back from Africa, and told me that you had had trouble with both him and his good-for-nothing son. He seems bound to shadow me wherever I go."

"But the Eclipse Mine—" broke in Dick.

"I am getting to that. Kennedy had left his interest in it to me, but Baxter claimed the whole discovery as his own, saying he was out on his own hook when the mine was located, which was a falsehood. But though Baxter claimed the mine he could not locate it, nor could I do so. It was along a creek which a certain Jack Wumble had called Bumble Bee, but we could not locate this creek, and Jack Wumble had departed for fresh fields. But I have located the old miner, and he has told me that Bumble Bee Creek was in reality one of the south branches of the Gunnison River, and is now called the Larkspur. You must remember that in those, early days matters were very unsettled in Colorado, and names changed almost weekly."

"So this Eclipse Mine is on Larkspur Creek?"

"Yes, at a point three hundred yards above a white cliff which the old miners used to call Rooney's Ghost, because a miner named Rooney once committed suicide there."

"And what about Baxter, father? If he has those papers, do you think he or his confederate will go up the Larkspur to locate the Eclipse Mine?"

"Undoubtedly—under another name—that is, if it proves as valuable as my old partner anticipated."

"But if we can get there before him and locate for ourselves?"

"Ah, if I could do that, Dick, then I would not fear Baxter or anybody else. But if he gets in ahead of me—well, you know, 'possession is nine points of the law,' and he can at least make me a lot of trouble."

Dick sprang from the seat into which he had dropped.

"He shan't do it, father!" he exclaimed.

"But how are you going to help it, my son? I cannot go West with this sprained ankle."

"I'll go West myself and locate that claim in spite of what Arnold Baxter has done."

"You go West?"

"Yes."

"Without me? That would be, a—well—"

"Remember, father, I went to Africa to find you."

"I shall never forget it, Dick. But you had others with you—your Uncle Randolph, and Tom, and Sam, and Aleck."

"Well, I can take Tom and Sam with me again, if it comes to that."

"It is a wild country out there among the mining camps of the mountains."

"It's no wilder than in the heart of Africa."

Mr. Anderson Rover shook his head doubtfully. "And then if Baxter found out what you were trying to do he would—" He could not finish, but Dick understood.

"I shall be on my guard, father. I know what a scoundrel he is, and will give him no chance to get at me."

At that point the conversation was interrupted by the hired girl, who came to call Dick to a late supper. The lad was hungry, so he did not refuse. By the time he had finished, Mr. Rover had gone to bed, so his son also retired, without probing the Eclipse Mine affair any further. But it was a long time before Dick got to sleep, so full was his head of the suddenly proposed trip to the West.

CHAPTER XVII
BOUND FOR THE WEST

On the following morning Tom and Sam arrived, as anxious as Dick had been to learn the particulars of what had occurred. They listened to their father's story with interest, as he told of how he had heard a noise and gone below to grapple with the midnight intruder who was ransacking the library desk, and of how Randolph Rover had come to his assistance and been seriously wounded, and how all were now certain that the unwelcome visitor had been Arnold Baxter—that is, all but Randolph Baxter, who lay semi-unconscious, in a high fever, and who knew nothing.

The doctor came in at noon, and pronounced Randolph Rover but little better.

"He must be kept very quiet," said the medical man. "Do not allow anybody to disturb him. If he should become in the least excited I would not answer for his life." So the boys kept away from his bed-chamber and walked about on tiptoes and spoke in whispers.

It was Dick who called together a council of war, out in the barn, late in the afternoon, after he had had another long talk with his father.

"Here's the whole thing in a nutshell," he said. "Arnold Baxter has those papers—or the best part of them—and he means to stake that claim if he can."

"But he won't dare to show himself," said Sam. "If he does, we can turn him over to the police."

"Of course he won't show himself, but he'll get somebody else to stake the claim and whack up," replied Dick.

"We won't let him do it," interposed Tom bluntly. "I'll go to Colorado myself and stop him."

"Good for you, Tom! You've struck the nail's head first clip," said his elder brother.

"Father was going out there this spring, anyway—and he was going to take us."

"True. Father would go to-day if he could, but he can't, on account of that hurt ankle," went on Dick.

"Then let us go for him," came from Sam. "We can do nothing here but worry Uncle Randolph, and I don't feel like going back to Putnam Hall while this excitement is on."

"I told father that I wanted to go, lout he is afraid the trip would be too dangerous."

"Pooh! we went to Africa," was Tom's comment. He was awfully proud of that trip to the Dark Continent.

"It isn't the trip so much as it is the fact that we may fall in with Arnold Baxter and his confederates."

"By the way, I wonder if Dan has joined his father?" mused Sam.

"Like as not. Certainly Dan knew what his parent was up to—sotherwise he wouldn't have written that letter Josiah Crabtree dropped."

"Then you can be sure the two Baxters have gone to Colorado," said Tom.

"And the three Rovers will go, too," said Sam.

"Will you?" asked Dick. "I wanted to say so, but—"

"Yes, we'll go, and that settles it," cried Tom. "And the sooner we get off the better. But we must get father to explain everything a little more closely before we leave."

It was easy to get Anderson Rover to explain, but not so easy to get him to consent to their going out to Colorado. At last he said that if they could get Jack Wumble to go with them they might go.

"Jack Wumble is all right, and if he says he will stick to you I know he will keep his word. He is a crack shot, and besides he knows Larkspur Creek from end to end, and it will save you a lot of hunting around to have him by to give information."

"And where can we find Jack Wumble?

"The last I heard of him he was in Chicago. He is rather a reckless man, and when he has money is apt to spend it in gambling. But his heart is true blue and honest to the core."

"Do you know where he was stopping?"

"At a hotel called the Western Palace. It is a great resort for mining men, and you will be sure to find out all about him if you ask for him there," concluded Mr. Rover.

A great deal more had to be talked about and considered, but we will pass that over. It was decided that the boys should leave for Chicago early on the following Monday morning. The spare time was used up in getting ready for the trip. The boys had their trunks shipped home from Putnam Hall, and wrote to the master and their friends telling of what was going on, but entering into no particulars. By Saturday night they were all ready, and on Sunday went to church at their aunt's request.

"I hate to see you go," said Mrs. Rover, with a sad smile. "It is a big risk. Be sure and come back safe and sound."

"We will," answered Tom. "And you be sure and have Uncle Randolph up and well when we do come back," he added. Poor Tom! little did he think of the grave perils that waited for him in the far West!

The day was a perfect one when they left, the air full of bright sunshine and the music of the birds which had made Valley Brook their summer home for many years. Mrs. Rover saw them to the carriage, while Anderson Rover waved them a serious adieu from his bedroom window. Poor Randolph Rover was as feverish as ever, and knew nothing of their coming or their going. All of the boys were half afraid they would never again see their uncle alive.

But youth is strong and hopeful, and by the time they had entered the cars and made themselves comfortable the scenes around them engrossed their attention, and the past was forgotten for the time being. The train was an express, and flew along at the rate of sixty miles an hour.

"We'll be in Chicago by this time to-morrow," said Dick. "It's quick traveling, isn't it?"

"I hope we are fortunate enough to catch Jack Wumble," said Tom. "I don't want to lose time in Chicago hunting him up."

The car was but half filled, so that the boys had several seats all to themselves. They had brought with them a map of Colorado, and they spent much of the day in studying this.

When it came time for dinner they entered the dining car. They could not get seats together, and so Tom was compelled to sit opposite to a burly fellow whose appearance did not strike him as altogether favorable.

"Bound for Chicago?" asked the man, after passing the time of day.

"Yes, sir," answered Tom. "Are you bound there?"

"I am going through that city. You belong there, I suppose?"

"No, sir, I've never been there before."

"Is that so. Going on a pleasure trip, or to try your luck? Or perhaps you are on business?"

"Yes, I am on business."

"You are rather young to be out on business, it strikes me," went on the burly stranger, after a pause.

"Oh, I've been around a little before," said Tom coolly.

"Yes, you look like a lad who has seen some thing of the world. Well, I've seen something of the world myself."

"Are you a Western man?" asked Tom, who thought it would not hurt to do a little questioning on his own account.

"Yes, I was born and brought up in Colorado."

The reply interested Tom.

"But you have traveled, you say?"

"Yes, I've been to San Francisco and to New York, and also up in the mining districts of the Northwest Territory, and in the mines of Mexico. I've been what they call a rolling stone." And the burly man laughed lightly, but the laugh was not a pleasant one.

"Then you ought to know a good deal about mining," Tom ventured. "I am interested in the mines of Colorado. In what part of the State were you located?"

"Well, I lived in Ouray some time, and also in Silverton, but I went here, there, and everywhere, prospecting and buying up old claims cheap."

"I hope you struck it rich."

"Oh, I'm fairly well fixed," was the careless answer. "So you are interested in our mines, eh? Got a claim?"

"No, sir, but I am going out there to look up a claim — if I can."

"Take my advice and leave mining alone unless you have had experience. The chance for a tenderfoot, as we call 'em, getting along has gone by."

"I shan't waste much time in looking around."

"And don't waste your money either. Nine mines out of ten that are offered for sale are not worth buying at any price. I've been all through the miff and I know."

"I suppose you know a great many of the old time miners?" said Tom, after another pause.

"Oh, yes, loads of them, Quray Frank, Bill Peters, Denver Phil, and all the rest."

"Did you ever meet a man by the name of Jack Wumble?"

The burly man started and spilled a little of the coffee he was holding to drink.

"Why — er — confound the rocking of the train," he answered. "Why, yes, I met Wumble once or twice, but never had any business with him. Are you going to buy a mine from him?"

"No, I am going to try to get him to help locate one that is missing," answered Tom, before he had thought twice.

"Indeed! Well, I've heard Jack is a good man at locating paying claims. Do you know him personally?"

"I do not."

A gleam of satisfaction lit up the burly man's face, but Tom did not notice it.

"Wumble used to hang out in Denver. Going to meet him there, I suppose."

"No, I'm going to meet him in Chicago, if I can."

"I see."

So the talk ran on until the meal was finished. Then the burly man bowed pleasantly and the two separated.

When Tom rejoined his brothers Sam asked him about the man.

"I'm sure I've seen him before," he said. "But where is more than I can say."

"I think I've seen him, too," said Dick. "And I must say I don't much like his looks."

When Tom told of the conversation that had been held, Dick shook his head seriously.

"I wouldn't talk so much, Tom," he remarked. "It won't do any good, and it may do harm, you know."

"I'll be more careful hereafter, Dick. I am sorry myself that I had so much to say," returned Tom.

CHAPTER XVIII
THE ROVER BOYS IN CHICAGO

"Chicago! Change cars for St. Louis and the West!"

The long express had rolled into the great depot and the porters were busy brushing up the passengers in the parlor cars and gathering together their baggage—and incidentally, the tips which were forthcoming.

The Rover boys were soon out on the platform and making for the street.

"Cab, sir; coupe?"

"Mornin' papers! All de news! Have a paper, boss?"

The crowd of newsboys and hackmen made Dick smile. "It's a good deal like New York, isn't it?" he observed.

"Yes, indeed," replied Sam. "Where shall we go—to the Western Palace?"

"We might as well. The sooner we find this Jack Wumble the better."

At that moment the burly man who had talked to Tom in the dining car brushed up to them.

"Good-morning, my young friend," he said to Tom. "Can I be of any assistance to you?"

"It I don't know as you can," replied Tom coldly. "I guess we can find our way around."

"Glad to help you if I can," went on the man.

"We want to get to the Western Palace," put in Sam, before his brothers could stop him.

"That is quite a distance from here." The man hesitated a moment. "I was going there myself. If you don't mind riding on a street car I'll show you the way."

"A street car is good enough for us," returned Sam. He was anxious to see more of the stranger, for he wished if possible to recollect where he had seen the fellow before.

A passing car was hailed and they all got on board, each carrying a valise, for the Rover boys had decided that trunks would be too cumbersome for the trip. They sat close together, and during the ride the stranger endeavored to make himself as agreeable as possible.

"My name is Henry Bradner," he said, introducing himself. "Out in the mines they used to call me Lucky Harry, and a good many of my friends call me that still. May I ask your names?"

"My name is Sam Rover," said the boy. "This is my brother Dick, and this my brother Tom."

There were handshakings all around. "Glad to know you," said Bradner. "I hope you find Jack Wumble and that he locates your mine for you."

"I've been thinking that I've seen you before," said Sam bluntly. "But for the life of me I can't place you."

"Perhaps we've met somewhere in the East — New York, for instance. Have any of you been in Chicago before?"

"No."

"It's a great city and there are many sights worth seeing. If you wished I wouldn't mind showing you around a bit this afternoon or tomorrow."

"Thanks, but we won't have time," said Dick shortly. This off-handed invitation made him more suspicious than ever.

The talking continued until at last Henry Bradner stopped the car.

"Here we are," he said. "The Palace of the West is one block down yonder side street."

"The Palace of the West?" repeated Tom. "I thought it was called the Western Palace."

"Well, it's all the same," laughed the man. But it was not the same by any means. While the Western Palace was a first-class hotel in every respect, the Palace of the West was a weak imitation, run by a man who had once been a notorious San Francisco blackleg.

The hotel was soon reached and Bradner led the way into the office, which was filled with rather rough-looking sports, all smoking and talking loudly.

"I know the clerk," said Bradner. "I'll ask him about your friend." And before Dick could stop him he had pushed his way to the desk and was talking in a low tone to the clerk. Dick tried to catch what was said, but was unable to do so.

"You are in luck," said Bradner, on coming back. "The clerk says Jack Wumble has gone off for the day, but said he would be back by to-night sure."

"I'm glad of that," said Tom, and he and his brothers felt much relieved.

"The clerk cautioned me to keep quiet about Wumble," went on Bradner confidentially. "It seems Wumble and another man had a row over a game of cards, and Wumble wants the other man to clear out before he shows up again. The other man is booked for Denver on the afternoon train."

As this statement about cards fitted in with what Mr. Rover had said concerning Jack Wumble, the boys swallowed it without hesitation, and they were inclined to believe that Henry Bradner was all right, after all.

"Will you register here?" went on the man.

"No, I don't like the looks of the place," answered Dick promptly. "We are not of the drinking kind," he added.

The burly man looked dark and disappointed.

"It's a good hotel, when once you get used to it," he said.

But Dick shook his head and said he would go elsewhere, and motioning to Tom and Sam he led the way to the sidewalk once more. Henry Bradner followed them.

"If I see Wumble shall I get him to wait for you?" he said.

"If you wish. We will be around to-night and also to-morrow morning to see him."

"All right."

The boys walked off and around the corner into the street where the cars were running.

"I don't like him at all," exclaimed Dick. "I believe he is tip to some game."

"Oh, you may be too suspicious," declared Sam. "What game can he be up to? He was kind enough to help us hunt up this Jack Wumble."

"I don't care—his manner doesn't suit me at all. He's a sneak, if ever there was one."

The boys walked on for a distance of several blocks, and then coming to a nice-looking restaurant went in for dinner.

While they were eating Dick happened to glance out of the show window of the place and gave a low cry.

"What is it, Dick?" asked Tom.

"I thought as much. That man is watching us."

Sam and Tom gave a look, but by this time Henry Bradner had disappeared from view.

"You are sure that you saw him, Dick?" asked Sam.

"I am positive. Boys, do you know what I think? I think he is a sharper, and imagines he has three green country boys with money to deal with."

"Well, if he thinks that he is much mistaken," was Tom's comment. "In the first place we are not so very green, and in the second our cash account is rather limited."

"We spoke about a mine, and he may imagine that we carry several thousands of dollars with us."

"If he's a sharper why did he try to find Wumble for us?" asked Sam.

This was a poser and Dick did not pretend to answer it.

The dinner finished, they walked forth once more and down into the heart of the city.

They soon found what looked to be a fairly good hotel, and engaged a large room with two beds for the night.

"Now we can take a look around," said Tom.

The best part of the afternoon was spent in sight-seeing, and the boys visited Lincoln Park, Jackson Park, the museum, menagerie, Masonic Temple, and numerous other points of interest.

They were returning to the hotel at which they had registered for the night when suddenly Tom caught his brothers by the arm.

"Well, I never!" he gasped. "What do you think of that?"

They saw he was gazing across the way, and looking in the direction saw an elegant hotel, over the broad doorway of which was stretched the sign:

WESTERN PALACE
GEORGE LAVELLE, Proprietor.
Established 1871.

"By jinks! That Bradner deceived us!" gasped Dick. "This must be the hotel father mentioned."

"But what about Jack Wumble?" began Sam. "He was registered at the other place."

"Did you see the register?" demanded Dick.

"No, but—"

"We'll soon learn the truth," went on the elder Rover. "Come on." And he made his way through the mass of moving wagons and trucks to the opposite side of the thoroughfare.

All entered the broad hallway together. The floor was of marble, and big mirrors lined every wall. Certainly the place was in sharp contrast to that known as the "Palace of the West."

Walking up to the office counter Dick inspected the register. On the third page from the last written upon he found the entry:

"Jack Wumble, Denver; Room 144."

"There, what do you think of that?" he demanded, as he showed his brothers the entry.

Both were dumfounded, and for the moment knew not what to say. Dick turned to one of the clerks.

"Is Mr. Jack Wumble in?" he asked.

The clerk looked at the row of keys behind him.

"No, sir; he's out."

"Have you any idea when he will be back?"

"I have not. Perhaps he is back already and over in the smoking room."

"I don't know him personally, but I am very anxious to see him."

"I'll have a boy look for him," returned the clerk, and called up a bell-boy, who took Dick's card and went off with it to the smoking room and the dining hall, calling softly as he passed one man and another, "Number 144! Number 144!"

Presently the bell-boy came back, followed by a tall, thin, and pleasant-faced man of sixty, wearing a light-checked suit and a broad-brimmed slouch hat.

"This is the gentleman, sir," he said to Dick.

"Are you Mr. Jack Wumble?" asked Dick curiously.

"That's my handle, lad," was the answer, in a broad, musical voice. "And I see your card reads Richard Rover. Any relation to Andy Rover, as used to be a mining expert?"

"I am his son."

"Well, well! His son, eh? Glad to know you, downright glad!" And Jack Wumble nearly wrung Dick's hand off. Then Tom and Dick were introduced, and more handshaking followed, and the boys felt that they had found a true friend beyond a doubt.

CHAPTER XIX
THE BURLY STRANGER'S LITTLE GAME

"I'm more than glad to have met you as we did," said Dick, a little later, after Jack Wumble had asked the boys about their father. "I think it has saved us from getting into a lot of trouble."

And he related the particulars of the meeting with Henry Bradner, and what the stranger had said and done concerning Wumble.

"The snake!" ejaculated the old miner passionately. "He's a sharp, true as you are born! Why, I never put up at the Palace of the West in my life."

"I wish I knew what his game was," went on Dick.

"You will know Dick—if I can get my hands on him. Do you reckon as how he is over to that other hotel now?"

"More than likely."

"Unless he shadowed us to here," burst out Tom. "If he did that he must know his game is up, and you can be sure he will keep out of sight."

The matter was talked over, and it was decided that Jack Wumble and the boys should go to the other hotel without delay.

On the way Dick told the old miner what had brought them to the West. Jack Wumble took a deep interest in all mining schemes, and listened closely to all the youth had to say.

"Yes, I remember about the Eclipse Mine," he said. "And I remember this Arnold Baxter, too. He was a bad one, and if I and some others had our say he would have dangled from a tree for his stealings, for, you see, we didn't have no jails in those days, and stealing was a capital crime."

"It will you help us to locate the mine before Arnold Baxter or his confederates can get on the ground? We will pay you for your trouble."

"Certainly, I'll do what I can. But I—don't want any of Anderson Rover's pile—not me. Why, your father nursed me through the worst case o' fever a miner ever had—an' I ain't forgittin' it, lads. I'll stick to ye to the end." And the old miner put out his hand and gave another squeeze that made Dick wince.

The Palace of the West reached, Wumble pushed his way into the smoke-laden office and to the desk.

"Say, is there a man named Jack Wumble stopping here?" he demanded.

"Jack Wumble," repeated the clerk slowly.

"That's what I said."

"There is a Jack Wimple stopping here—but he is out—gone to St. Louis."

"Jack Wimple? He's not the man," and the old miner fell back and repeated what had been said to the three boys.

"Perhaps Bradner made a mistake," suggested Tom. "But I don't believe it."

"He tried to make us believe this hotel and the Western Palace were one and the same," put in Sam.

"He's sharp, I tell you," declared Jack Wumble. "Just wait till I get on his trail, I'll make him tell us the truth. More than likely he wanted to clean you boys out."

They waited around for the best part of an hour, but Henry Bradner failed to return, and at last they gave up looking for him, and the boys went back to where they had hired a room for the night, promising to rejoin Jack Wumble early in the morning, when the whole party would take a train for Denver, where Wumble wished to transact a little business before starting out for Larkspur Creek.

The boys had not slept very well on the train, so they were thoroughly tired out. They were on the point of retiring when a bell-boy came up stating that their friend wished to see Dick for a few minutes.

"Wumble must have forgotten something," said Dick. "I'll see what it is," and he took the elevator to the ground floor.

To his surprise it was not Wumble who wished to see him, but Henry Bradner.

"What, you!" cried the youth. "I thought you had skipped out."

"Skipped out?" queried the burly man in pretended surprise. "Why should I skip out?"

"Don't you know that we have found you out?"

"Found me out? You are talking in riddles, young man." And the stranger drew himself up proudly.

"We have found Mr. Jack Wumble, and he tells us that he never stopped at the Palace of the West in his life."

"Mr. Jack Wimple, you mean. Why, he is certainly at the hotel — or was."

"We were looking for Mr. Wumble — and you know it. I care nothing for your Mr. Wimple. And besides, you told us that the Western Palace and the Palace of the West were one and the same. That was a deliberate falsehood."

Bradner turned pale, and looked as if he wished to catch Dick by the throat. "Have a care, young man!" he hissed. "I am not a man to be trifled with. I tried to do you a good turn, but I see I have put my foot into it. Henceforth you can take care of yourself."

So speaking, Henry Bradner turned on his heel and strode off, a look of baffled rage in his eyes. Instantly Dick turned to a bell-boy.

"Run up to room 233 and tell Tom Rover to come down at once and follow his brother," he said hurriedly. "I can't go up — I want to watch that man, for he's a crook."

The boy seemed to understand, and flew for the stairs, the elevator being out of sight. Dick ran to the door, to behold Bradner standing on the sidewalk as if undecided which way to pursue his course. But presently he walked slowly up the street. Dick followed him, and had gone less than half a block when Tom joined him, all out of breath with running.

"What is it, Dick?"

"It was Bradner, who came to smooth matters over. I am following him to see if I can't get on to his game."

"Oh, what nerve! I should think he would have been afraid to come near us."

"He's a bold one, Tom, and we must look out that we don't get bit by him."

Henry Bradner covered half a dozen blocks of the street upon which the hotel was located, and then turned into a narrow thoroughfare running toward the Chicago river.

Here were a number of low drinking places, and in front of one of these he stopped. Instead of entering the resort by the main door he went in through a side hallway, which led to a rear room.

"Perhaps he is stopping here," suggested Tom, as the two lads came to a halt.

"Well, if that is so we had better remember the place," answered Dick.

There was an alleyway alongside of the house, and looking into this the boys saw a light shining out of several windows near the rear of the resort.

"Let us take a peep into the windows," suggested Dick, and led the way.

To let out some of the tobacco smoke the windows were pulled down partly from the top. The bottom sashes were covered with half-curtains of imitation lace, but so flimsy that the boys saw through them without difficulty.

Bradner had just entered this rear room, and was gazing around inquiringly. Now he stalked over to a table near one of the windows, and dropped heavily into a chair.

"I'm afraid the jig is up," he said, addressing somebody on the opposite side of the table.

"What has happened," asked the other person, and now the two Rover boys were amazed to learn that the party was Dan Baxter. The bully had changed his dress and also the style of wearing his hair, and was sporting a pair of nose glasses.

"They have met the real Jack Wumble, and found out that I was fooling them about the hotel."

"That's too bad," cried Dan Baxter. "You must have made a bad break of it, Bradner."

"I did my best, but I couldn't keep them from looking around, although I offered to conduct them. You can bet if I had had them under my care they wouldn't have got near the Western Palace, nor Jack Wumble either."

"Did you have a man ready to play the part of Wumble?" questioned Dan Baxter, after the burly one had ordered drinks for the two.

"Yes, I had Bill Noxton all cocked and primed. But now our cake is dough—and after all the trouble I've taken for your father, too!" And Henry Bradner uttered a snort of disgust.

"Did you warn this Noxton?"

"Oh, yes, and I put a flea into the ear of the hotel clerk, too. But the thing is, what do you suppose your father will want done next?"

"Don't ask me," answered Dan Baxter recklessly. "He don't half trust me any more. He says I'm only good to sponge on him," and the former bully of Putnam Hall gave a bitter laugh.

"Well, I haven't followed these Rovers all the way from Valley Brook farm to here for nothing," went on Henry Bradner. "Your father wanted 'em watched, and I've watched 'em ever since they came home from that boarding academy. It was a big job, too."

"Didn't they suspect you?"

"One of 'em said he thought he had seen me before." And Bradner laughed. "It was at the Valley Brook Church. I followed them to the church just to keep my word to your father."

"And you are certain Mr. Rover isn't coming West?"

"No, he's laid up with a game leg, and won't move for a month. I got that straight from the hired man." There was a pause. "What do you reckon I had best do next?"

"Telegraph to my father at Denver—you know his assumed name, and let him advise you. I suppose the boys and that Wumble will go straight through to the mining district now."

"More than likely."

"Then father and Roebuck will have to stop them out there, although how it's to be done I don't know."

At this juncture a waiter came forward, and closed down the window, and the balance of the conversation was lost to the two Rover boys.

CHAPTER XX
JUST A LITTLE TOO LATE

"What do you think of that?" whispered Dick, as he led the way back to the sidewalk.

"It's all as plain as day," replied his brother. "This Bradner was set to watch the house immediately after the robbery occurred. More than likely he was around at the time of the robbery."

"Do you suppose he is the man who helped Arnold Baxter to escape from prison on that forged pardon?"

"Creation! It may be so!" ejaculated Tom. "I'll tell you one thing: we ought to have them both arrested at once."

"I don't know about that," mused the elder Rover. "If we do that then how are we to find out where Arnold Baxter is, or this fellow they called Roebuck?"

"But they may slip through our fingers if we don't have them locked up."

The two brothers talked the matter ever, and then decided, late as it was, to call upon Jack Wumble for advice.

"You can go for him," said Dick. "I'll continue to watch this place. If they leave I'll throw bits of paper on the sidewalk and you can follow the trail just as if we were playing a game of hare and hounds."

Tom made off at top speed, carefully noting the street and number, so that he would not miss his way when returning.

Left to himself Dick went into the alleyway again and looked through the window as before.

Dan Baxter and Bradner were still conversing, but the youth could not hear what was said.

Presently the pair at the table arose, settled for their drinks and came out of the place.

They walked up the street and around a corner, and Dick followed, scattering bits of an old letter as he went along. When the letter was used up, he tore to bits some handbills which he found in the street.

Eight squares were covered before Dan Baxter and Bradner reached a dingy looking hotel which went by the name of Lakeman's Rest.

It was set in the middle of the block, with brick houses on either side of it.

They entered a narrow hallway, and by the light above the door Dick saw them ascend the stairs to the second floor.

There now seemed nothing to do but to await Tom's return, and the youth retired to the opposite side of the street.

It was late—after midnight, in fact—and the street was practically deserted.

A half hour went by and Dick felt as if his brother would never return, when he heard swift footsteps behind him.

"So this is your game, eh?" cried the voice of Bradner, and of a sudden a club descended upon Dick's head and he went down as if shot.

The man had looked out of the hotel window and spotted Dick, and had gone out by a back way add around the square to make certain of his victim.

"That was a good crack," came from Dan Baxter. "It serves him right for following you."

Bradner was about to bend over his victim to ascertain how badly Dick was hurt when the footsteps of two men approaching made him draw back.

"Come, we don't want to be caught," whispered Dan Baxter nervously.

And then, as the footsteps came closer, he darted away, with Henry Bradner at his heels. They did not stop until a long distance away from the scene of the dastardly attack.

The men who were approaching were a couple of bakers who were employed in a neighboring bakery.

"Vas ist dis!" cried one of them, as he stumbled over Dick's body. "A young mans!"

"He is drunk, Carl," said the other. "Let him be or you may get into trouble."

"Maype he vos hurt, or sick," said the German baker, bending down. "I vos know der cop on dis beat and he knows I vos no footpad."

Just then Dick gave a shiver and a groan, and both bakers realized that he was suffering in some way. While the German remained by the boy's side the other ran to the bakery for a lantern and assistance.

Soon a small crowd had collected, and Dick was carried into the bakery and made as comfortable as the means permitted. One of the bakers went on a hunt for a policeman, and presently the officer of the law hove into sight. Dick was just coming to his senses, but was too dazed for several minutes to give an account of what had happened. At last he said a man had struck him down with a club.

"Were you robbed?" asked the policeman.

Dick felt in his various pockets.

"No, sir."

"You were lucky."

"I dink ve scare der rascal avay," said the German baker.

"More than likely. It's a pity you didn't collar him." The policeman turned to Dick.

"Shall I call up an ambulance?"

"I don't think it's necessary, sir. My brother will be along this way soon. I was waiting for him to come when I was struck."

"You were out rather late," remarked the officer of the law, suspiciously.

"I was watching a rascal who tried to make trouble for me."

"Then there must be more to this case than what you just told me."

"There is."

"In that case you had better go to police headquarters with me."

"I am willing. But won't you wait until my brother gets here?"

There was no need to wait, for at that moment Tom appeared on the scene, accompanied by Jack Wumble. They both stared at Dick in horror.

"Oh, Dick, you are hurt?" cried Tom.

"Not very much. Bradner hit me on the head. I am glad I am alive."

"And where is the rascal now?" questioned the old miner.

"Ran away."

"And Dan Baxter?" queried Tom.

"Gone, too, I suppose. They must have been together." And then Dick related what had occurred—so far as he knew—since Tom had left him.

The officer of the law accompanied all three to the police station, and here the boys told their story, and a watch was set for Bradner and Dan Baxter. But nothing came of this, for the pair left Chicago early the next day.

"We had better keep close together after this," said Jack Wumble, as he was seeing the boys back to their hotel. "I reckon you've got a mighty bad crowd to deal with." And he remained with them for the balance of the night.

The express for Denver left at eleven o'clock in the morning, and all of the party of four were on hand to catch it. Soon they were whirling over the fields and through the forests toward the mighty Mississippi River.

"Never been West afore-eh?" remarked Jack Wumble. "Well, you will see some grand sights, I can tell ye that."

"No, we have never been West," answered Sam. "But we have been to Africa," he added proudly.

"Gee shoo! is that so! Well, that's long traveling certainly. But I reckon I'd rather see my own country first."

"We went to Africa for a purpose," said Tom, and told of the rescue of his father. The old miner listened with keen appreciation and at the conclusion clapped Tom on the back.

"You're true blue, Tom!" he cried. "You and your brothers will pull through, I feel sure of it." And then he fell to telling about his own life, and how he had become acquainted with Anderson Rover and his partner Kennedy, and of the various bad things Arnold Baxter had done in those days. "This man seems to be a chip of the old block," he concluded.

The trip to Denver was full of interest, and Dick was sorry he did not have a camera along, that he might take snapshots of the scenery. Yet he was impatient to get to his destination and stake out the missing Eclipse Mine before Arnold Baxter and his confederates should have the chance to do so.

It was the afternoon of the next day when Denver was reached, and a light rain was falling. Jack Wumble wished to put up at a hotel called the Miner's Rest, a favorite resort with men from the mining districts. He had been negotiating for the sale of one of his mines, and thought he could close the deal the next morning.

"And then we'll be off for Larkspur Creek without further delay," was what he told Dick.

CHAPTER XXI
OFF FOR THE MINING DISTRICT

While Jack Wumble was off attending to his private business the three Rover boys took a stroll through Denver.

The city was different from any they had visited, and their walk was full of interest.

Coming to a store in the window of which were exhibited a number of Indian curiosities, the boys halted to examine the objects, when Tom uttered a sudden cry.

"Look, Dick! There is Bradner inside!"

"Yes, and Dan Baxter is with him!" returned the elder brother quickly. "Here's luck, surely!"

"Will you have them locked up?" asked Sam.

"To be sure—if we can."

The boys looked around for a policeman, but none happened to be in sight.

"Run and see if you can find one," said Dick to Sam. "Tom and I can watch the pair."

At once Sam made off. But policemen were not numerous, and it took quite some time to locate one and explain what was wanted.

In the meantime Dan Baxter had caught sight of Tom and told Bradner of his discovery.

Boy and man came out of the store in a great hurry. They were about to run off when Dick caught Bradner by the arm, while his brother halted the former bully of Putnam Hall.

"Let go of me!" hissed Bradner, and as Dick paid no attention he aimed a blow for the youth's head. But Dick "had been there before," and dodged, and the force of his effort nearly took the rascal off his feet. Before he could recover Dick had him down on his back and was sitting on his chest.

Tom was having a lively time with Dan Baxter. The bully hit the boy in the shoulder, and Tom retaliated with a sharp crack that landed straight on Baxter's nose and drew blood.

"A fight! a fight!" yelled a passing newsboy, and as if by magic a crowd began to collect.

Again Baxter struck out, but his blow fell short, and now Tom gave him one in the ear that spun him half around. By this time the bully felt that he had had enough of the encounter, and breaking through the crowd he set off on a mad run down the street and around the nearest comer.

Feeling it would be useless to try to catch Dan Baxter just then, Tom turned his attention to Dick and Henry Bradner. Bradner was struggling hard to get up, but Dick was master of the situation, so Tom had little to do.

"What's the meaning of this?" demanded the policeman, as soon as he came upon the scene.

"I want this man arrested," answered Dick, as he got up, but still kept close to Bradner.

"What has he done?"

"He is a sharper of the worst kind."

"You are sure of this?"

"I am—"

"You will have to go to the station house with us if I take the man in," continued the policeman.

"I am willing," answered Dick quietly.

Muttering angrily to himself, Henry Bradner arose. He wanted to run away, but got no chance to do so. Soon the station house was reached, and here Dick and his brothers told their story.

"The assault happened in another State," said the officer at the desk. "The most we can do is to hold him until the Illinois authorities send for him."

"Why, that's Harry the Crook, from Gunnison!" put in an officer who had just come in. "He is wanted here on half a dozen charges."

At these words Bradner turned deadly pale.

"This is a—a mistake," he faltered. "I know nothing of the man you mention."

"Too thin, Harry; I know you well," replied the officer. "Captain, he is a bad one," he continued to his superior.

An investigation into the records was made, and a picture in the Rogues' Gallery proved that Bradner and Harry the Crook were one and the same beyond a doubt.

"In that case we'll hold him right here," said the police captain.

The matter was talked over with Dick, and the youth decided to let his own charge against the crook drop, as he did not wish to waste time in Denver on the case. An hour later the three Rovers departed, leaving Henry Bradner to a fate he richly deserved.

"That is one of our enemies disposed of," observed Dick, as they walked back to the hotel. "I wish we could do up the Baxters just as easily."

The following day found them on the way to Gunnison. Nothing more had been seen or heard of Dan Baxter, nor had anything turned up concerning Arnold Baxter and Roebuck, the man who was with him and who hid helped him to escape from prison.

The country was now mountainous in the extreme, with here and there a wild, weird canyon thousands of feet deep. Some of the awful pitfalls made Sam fairly hold his breath.

"Gosh!" he murmured. "This beats Africa, doesn't it? Who ever saw such lofty peaks before—and such rivers cut out of the solid rock!"

The boys found Gunnison a small mining city containing perhaps six thousand souls. A few of the buildings were quite up to date, but the majority were little better than shanties. But Gunnison was a center for the trade of many miles around, and business was brisk.

At Gunnison the entire party procured horses from a dealer Jack Wumble knew, beasts that were strong and used to mountain traveling.

"We might go on for twenty miles or so by rail, but this is the best place for fitting out," said the old miner. "We can strike a putty fair trail from here, leading directly, to Larkspur Creek."

"And how far is that mining district from here?" asked Tom.

"As the birds fly about sixty-five miles. But the trail makes it a good hundred miles, and some putty stiff climbin' at that. I'm glad ye are used to roughin' it, for this traveling don't go well with a tenderfoot."

The day was clear and the air bracing, and the boys started off with their friend in the best of spirits. Soon the city was left behind, and then began a journey along the foothills which seemed to have no end.

"If Arnold Baxter is watching us he is taking precious good care to keep out of sight," said Tom, as they rode along in single file, with Jack Wumble in the lead.

"No doubt Dan has joined his father and told him of Bradner's fate," returned Dick. "But we have got to keep our eyes wide open. We all know what a wretch Arnold Baxter is, and out in this wild country almost anything is liable to happen."

On and on they went, first over a stubble of thin grass and then through a forest of tall pine trees. Rocks were everywhere, and the trail wound in and out, with an occasional watercourse to be forded.

"These watercourses are all right now," observed Jack Wumble. "But in the early spring, when the snow on the mountains begins to melt, they become raging torrents, and getting across 'em is out of the question."

"How far are yonder peaks from here?" asked Sam, pointing ahead.

"About twenty miles."

"Gracious, as far as that! I didn't know one could see so clearly for such a long distance. They look to me to be only about three miles."

"The air is very pure and clear out here, lad. No better air in this wide world than that of Colorady."

At noon they came to a halt in a little hollow, protected alike from the breeze and the direct rays of the overhead sun. Their saddle bags were filled with provisions, and Tom and Sam began to prepare their first meal in the open, with Dick and the old miner assisting.

After the meal Jack Wumble took a smoke and a ten minutes' nap, and during that time the three boys strolled off in various directions, Sam going ahead on the trail.

Presently the youngest Rover had his eye arrested by a post set up in the middle of the trail. To the top of the post was tacked a sheet of white paper.

"This is queer," thought Sam, and drew closer to inspect the sheet. On it were written the words, in pencil:

"To the Rovers and their friend:

"If you want to keep out of trouble you will return to Gunnison at once. If you dare to push on to Larkspur Creek it may cost you your lives. We are watching you, and are fully armed, and you had better be warned in time.

"THE RIGHTFUL OWNERS OF THE MINE"

CHAPTER XXII
LOST IN THE MOUNTAINS

"Dick! Tom! Jack! Come here and see what I have found!"

Sam's cry was a loud one, and soon the others came up on a run, Jack Wumble pistol in hand, for his life in the open had taught him to be forever prepared for danger.

"Wot is it, lad?" asked the old miner anxiously.

"It's a quit notice for us," answered Sam soberly. "I can tell you, the Baxters mean to carry matters with a high hand."

All of the others read the notice in silence. Then Dick thrust his hands into his pockets coolly.

"I'll see them hanged before I'll go back," he said.

"I am with you," added Tom. "But we must be cautious after this, or the Baxters will be firing at us from an ambush."

"If only we could catch sight of them," put in Sam. "They ought to be shot on sight!"

The boys looked at Jack Wumble, who had remained silent.

"Do you advise us to go back?" asked Dick hastily.

"I can't say as I do, lads," was the slow response. "Yet it might be better to do that nor to be shot down and have yer body thrown into a canyon," added Wumble, speaking in his old time vernacular. "Perhaps your father would rather have ye back."

"I don't believe it," burst out Tom. "Father never wanted cowards for sons."

Dick caught the paper, tore it down and ripped it in two, throwing it to the wind.

"I say I'm going ahead."

"So am I," came from both of his brothers. "But you need not go Jack." went on Dick. "We don't wish you to run into danger, and—"

"Hold up, Dick, I said I would see ye through, and I will," cried the old miner. "But I want ye to realize what ye are doing, that's all. If you are shot down it will be yer own fault, so to speak."

"But we don't intend to be shot down," interrupted Tom. "We have run up against the Baxters before, so we know how to be careful."

"It aint like as if they were in a city in the East," went on the old miner. "Here some men are mighty free with their shootin'-irons. And they could take a shot at ye from a long distance, with a good rifle."

Thus talking the entire party walked back to their camp and sat down to discuss the situation in detail.

"Perhaps we had better not advance until dark," said Dick. "If we advance now we will simply be making targets of ourselves," and he shivered in spite of himself.

"We won't advance at all," put in Jack Wumble briefly. "We would be wuss nor fools if we did—with them human wildcats a—watchin' of us," and he began to puff vigorously at his short stump of a briarroot pipe.

"But you said—" began Tom, when the old miner waved him to silence.

"Let me think it out, lads, and then I'll tell ye my plan. We'll trick 'em—that's best," and he began to smoke again.

Satisfied that Jack Wumble knew the ground to be covered better than they did, the boys decided to let him have his own way, so long as the object of the expedition should be advanced. They sat down in the shade to rest, and thus several hours passed, and the old miner smoked up half 'a dozen pipefuls of his favorite plug mixture.

"I've got it," he cried at last. "If we kin work the deal we'll keep 'em guessing." And he laughed softly to himself.

His plan was a simple one. Several miles back on the trail there was a fork, the second trail running to the northward. His plan was to ride back to the fork, and then in the darkness of the night to take to the second trail.

"That don't lead to Larkspur Creek," he said. "But it leads to Go Lightly Gulch, and from there I know an old Indian trail which leads to the Larkspur by way of Bender Mountain. It's dangerous trail to ride, but it's safe, too, so far as our enemies are concerned, for they can't cover it from any other part of the mountains. They would either have to be right in front of us or right behind, and in that case we'd have as much of a show at them as they would have at us."

"That's a good plan," exclaimed Dick. "Let us adopt it, by all means."

Slowly the afternoon wore away, until the sun was lost to view behind the great Rocky Mountains in the west. As soon as the shadows became long and deep Jack Wumble arose.

"Now I reckon we can begin to ride on the back trail," he said, with a shrewd smile on his rugged face.

It was an easy matter to saddle the horse again.

The rest had made the animals as fresh as ever and this was a good thing, as the old miner calculated to ride a long distance between sunset and sunrise.

"I suppose our enemies are watching every move we make," said Tom.
"But I must say I can't catch a single glance of them."

"I thought I saw a speck or two of something over the hill to the south," said Dick.

Jack Wumble nodded. "You are right, Dick, I saw the specks too, and they were men looking in this direction. But they might not have been our enemies."

"If only we had a good field glass," sighed Sam. "I was going to bring one along, but I forgot all about it."

They rode on slowly, the old miner not wishing to reach the fork in the trail until it was quite dark. Fortunately it was clouding up, so that not even the stars would be left to betray them.

"We are coming to the fork," said Wumble, about eight o'clock. "Keep your eyes peeled, lads, and if you see anything out of the ordinary, let me know at once."

There was a tiny stream to cross, and then the way led around a series of sharp rocks.

"Keep to the grass as much as possible," cautioned the old miner in a voice that was a mere whisper. "And now follow me as fast as you can!"

Away he bounded in the lead, and the three Rover boys followed around the rocks through a stretch of pines and over some fallen firs, and then up and up a rugged trail where the footing was so insecure that the horses slipped continually. The branches of the drooping trees bothered them greatly, and had it not been for Wumble's continual warnings one or another of them would have been seriously hurt. The horses panted for breath, but still the old miner kept the pace until the top of the first range of foothills was gained. Here he called a halt under an overhanging rock beneath which it was as black as a dungeon.

"So far so good," he muttered, as he leaped to the ground and began to pat his heaving and perspiring animal. "I don't believe they know much about where we went to, even if they followed us back to the fork."

"I don't believe they are following us," said Dick, as he placed his ear to the ground and listened. All was as silent as the grave.

They remained under the rock the best part of an hour, allowing their trusty animals to get back their wind and strength. During this time Wumble walked back a short distance and Tom climbed up to the top of the rock, but neither made any discovery of importance.

It was a little after midnight when they moved forward again. Their pace was now little better than a walk, for the trail was a dangerous one, and in many spots they had to leap down and lead their horses. Once they came to a gully six to eight feet wide, without a bridge, and it took a good deal of urging to get Tom's horse to make the leap across.

"If a fellow should tumble in there where would he go to?" asked Sam, with a shudder.

"He'd go out of sight forever," replied Wumble solemnly. "Some of those cuts are a thousand feet deep."

"What a mighty upheaval of nature there must have been here at one time," said Dick.

By three o'clock in the morning Tom was completely fagged out and could scarcely keep his eyes open. Gradually he dragged behind the others, his eyes closing every few minutes in spite of his efforts to keep them open.

"I wish I had a cup of strong coffee to keep me awake," he murmured. "How much further are you going, Jack?"

"A couple of miles or so," answered the old miner. "Want a smoke? You can have my pipe."

"Thank you, but I don't smoke, and I guess it would only make me feel worse," answered Tom.

He began to drop further and further behind. The other boys spoke to him, but they were in reality nearly as much worn out as their brother, and had all they could do to keep Wumble in sight.

At last Tom's head fell forward on his breast, and on the instant he went fast asleep. His horse continued to move forward, but coming to a fork in the trail, took the downward path, that being the easier to travel. On and on went the beast, until striking a smooth road he set off on a gallop.

The violent motion aroused Tom, and he stared about him in bewilderment. "Dick! Sam!" he called out. "Where are you?"

No answer came back, and he sat bolt upright in alarm. Nobody was in sight, nor could he hear a sound saving the hoof beats of his own horse. He drew rein instantly.

"Dick!" he called loudly. "Jack Wumble! Where are you?"

Not a sound came in reply—not even the cry of a bird—all was absolutely silent. Tom gave something of a gasp. He realized his position only too well.

He was lost in the mountains.

CHAPTER XXIII
TOM MEETS THE ENEMY

"Oh, what a fool I was to fall asleep!"

Thus spoke poor Tom to himself, as he continued to gaze around him and call out. To one side was the high mountain, to the other a deep valley filled with giant trees, and on both sides an utter loneliness which seemed to penetrate his very soul.

Like a flash there came over him the various stories he had heard of men being lost in these mountains and wandering around for days and weeks until their very reason forsook them. Was he, too, doomed to such a horrible fate?

Fervidly he prayed to Heaven that such an ending might not overtake him. Then with care he turned his horse about, thinking to gain the point where he had become separated from the rest, and feeling that they must, sooner or later, turn back to look for him.

Once he imagined that he heard somebody calling him. But the sound was so far away he was not sure, and the echo was such that he could not determine from what direction the call emanated. Yet he yelled in return, nearly splitting his throat in his endeavor to make himself heard. For the time being the enemy was completely forgotten.

Tom's turning back, as he thought he was doing, only made matters worse, for the horse branched off on another trail—but so slender that it soon gave out altogether and left him on the trackless mountain side, and several miles from the fork where his steed had made the first mistake.

Yet he pressed on, calling again and again, but receiving no answer. Twice he imagined he heard pistol shots, and this gave him the idea of firing his own weapon, and he emptied the cylinder, but with no good to himself. Then he reloaded and came to a dead stop. He had never been more lonely in his life.

The balance of the night dragged so slowly that Tom thought it would never come morning again. With the first streak of light in the East he arose from the rock upon which he had thrown himself, and running to a higher point gazed eagerly around him.

He felt as Robinson Crusoe must have done on his deserted island. On all sides were rocks and hills, mountains and valleys, some bare and others covered with growths of pines and firs. Here and there glistened a rushing stream or a lofty waterfall, and on one of the hills he saw a herd of mule deer and on another a solitary Rocky Mountain goat. But nowhere was there the first sign of a human being.

Tom stood there for fully ten minutes, his breast heaving and his heart sinking within him like a lump of lead. He was alone, absolutely alone, in that wild and almost trackless region.

What was to be done?

Over and over he asked himself the question, and the answer always remained a blank. He knew not which way to turn, for going on might bring him into worse difficulty.

And yet he could not think of remaining still where he was, for the very thought was maddening. He must try to do something, be the consequence what it might.

Then he realized that his mouth was dry and that he was hungry. This made him remember that all of the provisions were loaded on the horses ridden by Jack Wumble and Dick. His own steed bore only some mining tools.

"I wish I could swap the tools for something to eat," he mused. "But there is no use in crying over spilt milk. I'm in a pickle, and I must do my best to get myself out of it."

At a short distance he saw a small hollow which had become partly filled by the rain of several days before. He walked to the hollow and drank his fill and then led his horse thither.

"We're lost, old man," he said, patting the beast on the neck. "We must find the others. You'll help, won't you?" And the horse pricked up his ears and looked around wisely as if he understood every word. At that moment Tom felt that a horse is indeed man's best friend.

He soon set off, but slowly, trying to locate the trail which had brought him astray, and trying at the same time, by the rising sun, to determine the direction in which his brothers and Jack Wumble had passed. But, as before, his efforts were misleading, and by the middle of the forenoon he found himself on a barren hilltop with no chance of leaving it excepting by the way he had come.

It was truly disheartening, and hot, tired, and discouraged he leaped again to the ground. He was now very hungry, without a morsel to satisfy the cravings of his stomach. His steed, too, wanted for something to eat, and gnawed eagerly at the spare vegetation as soon as permitted.

Tom was wondering what should be his next move when he was startled by the appearance of a mule deer on the hillside just below him. As he gazed at the animal he soon saw another, and then another, until the hillside seemed to be covered with them.

"I suppose men never come here to disturb them," he thought bitterly. "I wonder if I could bring one down with my pistol? I've got matches, and cooked deer's meat would be first class."

He crept as close as he could to the deer. Fortunately the breeze was blowing up the hill toward him, so the animals could not scent him readily. When he had gotten as near as he thought possible, he took careful aim and blazed away twice in quick succession.

His first shot was a failure, but his second landed in the deer's front leg, breaking that member at the knee and pitching the deer headlong. At once the rest of the herd took alarm, and went off like the wind, down the hillside into the valley and up another hill a good mile away. At the same time the wounded beast tried to rise, but before it could do so Tom ran closer and put three more balls into it, and then it rolled over, gave a jerk or two, and remained quiet forever.

The sight of such a feast made Tom's heart much lighter, and he brought out his pocket-knife and cut out some of the steaks. Then he moved down the hillside to where some brush promised abundant firewood and better forage for his horse.

The fire was soon lit and blazing away merrily, and the boy began to broil his steaks.

"Perhaps Dick and the others will see the smoke," he thought. "I trust they do, for I don't want to put in a whole night alone."

Tom ate his meal slowly, for he did not know what to do after it was finished. He wished he knew how far the nearest settlement was and in what direction.

After he had eaten his fill, he tied the balance of the steaks in a corner of his blanket, for the food must be kept for future use. Then he walked up to the top of the hill for another look around.

Suddenly he caught sight of a man riding swiftly toward him—a heavy-set man, with busky whiskers and a face that was almost black from constant exposure to the elements.

"Hullo, youngster!" cried the man, when he was within hailing distance. "All alone here?"

"I am!" cried Tom, and he felt something of joy to see a human being again.

"What brought you away out here? Hunting?"

"Not exactly, although I did bring down yonder animal," with a jerk of the thumb toward the deer. "I've lost my way."

"Did you, really? That's bad. It's lucky I ran across you. What's your handle?"

"Tom Rover," answered the youth boldly. "What is yours?"

"Noxton. So you are all alone?"

"Yes." Tom was trying to think where he had heard that name, but could not remember.

"Are you alone?"

"Well, hardly." Bill Noxton hesitated for a moment. "I was alone, but day before yesterday I fell in with a couple of Englishmen who are out here to see the sights, and they hired me to show 'em around. Our camp is just below here. Will you come down an' be introduced to the beef-eaters?"

"I suppose I might as well," answered Tom, never suspecting any trick. "I certainly don't want to remain alone any longer."

"Then come on. I told the beef-eaters I would be back inside of half an hour."

The man waited for Tom to mount, and then led the way down the hillside and into the valley. There was a patch of forest to pass, and they came out in a clearing on another hill, overlooking a mountain stream which flowed a hundred feet below.

"Here we are," cried Bill Noxton, as he suddenly wheeled behind Tom. "Shall I introduce you, Mr. Rover?"

Tom looked ahead, and his heart dropped.

There around a camp-fire sat Arnold Baxter and his son Dan, and a man who was a stranger to him. Clearly he was trapped, and in the hands of the enemy.

CHAPTER XXIV
THE SEARCH FOR THE MISSING BOY

"Tom isn't here!"

It was Dick who uttered the words, as of a sudden he wheeled around on the dark trail and tried to penetrate the blackness of night behind them.

"Isn't here?" demanded Jack Wumble, while Sam set up a cry of dismay.

"No. Tom! Tom!"

Sam joined in the cry, and so did the old miner, but as we already know, it was useless.

"This is the wust yet!" growled Jack Wumble. "I told ye all to keep close to me."

"Perhaps he fell asleep— I know he was dead tired," answered Dick, hitting the plain truth.

"We'll have to go back for him," said Sam, and turned without delay, for going ahead without Tom was all out of the question.

"Yes, we'll go back," rejoined the old miner. "But go slow, or you may make matters wuss. I kin follow a clear trail, even of three hosses, but I can't follow a trail mixed up backward an' forward."

They rode back slowly until at least half a mile had been covered. Then they shouted, but only a dismal echo came back. Dick fancied once that he heard Tom calling, but was not sure.

Daylight found them still searching around, Dick and Sam with more sober faces than they had worn in many a day. They knew only too well the danger of becoming lost in those wild mountains.

"Perhaps he has fallen in with Baxter's party," suggested Dick, as they came to a halt at the edge of a cliff overlooking a rushing river far below. It was past the breakfast hour, yet none of them felt like eating.

"Be careful how you expose yourself," observed Jack Wumble, as he screened himself and his horse behind some brush. "It won't do no good to Tom to let your enemies see you."

"If only we hadn't lost the trail," sighed Sam. The back trail had disappeared, on some rocks half an hour before and all efforts to take it up again had proved unsuccessful.

The Rover boys felt very much disheartened. Without Tom what was the use of going ahead to locate the missing mine?

"He's worth a dozen mines," said Dick.

"We must find him — we simply must."

But they were "stumped," to use Sam's way of expressing it, and with nothing better to do, Jack Wumble drew further back into the bushes, tethered his horse and got out the provisions for a meal. The boys ate mechanically and were soon done. Then Wumble got out his pipe and began to smoke more vigorously than ever.

"If we had a field glass we might spot him," he observed. "He can't be such a terrible distance away."

"I'm going to fire my pistol again," said Dick, and did, so, but no response came back and he re-loaded as crestfallen as ever.

It was a clear day, but the very sun seemed a mockery as it beamed down upon them.

"Supposing we separate and renew the hunt?" suggested Sam, but Wumble slowly shook his head.

"None o' that, lad. It will only be a case of another one lost. No, we must keep within sight of each other, no matter what we do. Come, I have an idea of looking into the valley on the other side of this hill, and then we can try the hill yonder."

Anything was better than sitting still, and once more they rode on. For the time being the enemy was almost forgotten.

They were going down along the edge of the cliff when, without warning, Dick's horse began to slip, having stepped on a rock which was insecure.

"Hi! whoa!" yelled the youth, and tried to hold the horse back. Then, as he saw the animal could not save himself, he leaped for the ground. The horse managed to scramble to a place of safety, but Dick, in trying to avoid a dangerous hoof stroke from the beast, lost his balance and went crashing down into the bushes overhanging the cliff!

Down and down, and still down, went the elder Rover, from one bush to another, his clothing catching here and there, thus partly staying his progress. But he could not stop himself entirely, and reaching the stream at last he went in with a loud splash and disappeared from view!

"Dick's gone!" ejaculated Sam. He tried to look over the edge of the cliff. "Oh, my! He will be drowned!"

He had heard the splash, as had also Wumble, and now both dismounted with all speed and crept to the very edge of the bushes. But the cliff bulged outward just below them and they could see nothing but a strip of the water on the opposite side.

"Dick! Dick!" sang out the brother. "Are you safe?"

No reply came back, and Sam's face turned white as he looked at Jack Wumble. "Do you think he has been — been killed?" The question nearly choked him.

"I can't say, Sam," was the answer. "We must git down an' see."

With extreme care the old miner let himself down from one clump of brush to another. His experience at prospecting stood him in good stead, for he had frequently climbed down just such heights to see if the mountain stream below would "pan out" sufficiently to set up a claim.

In the meanwhile Dick had gone to the very bottom of the stream, struck on the sand and rocks, and come up again. In falling down he had turned over and over, and he was as much dazed by this as he was by the quantity of cold water which he swallowed. For the minute after coming up he did not realize his situation. Then he felt himself borne along swiftly, he knew not to where. The rushing of the water was deafening, for the stream was approaching a narrow canyon, and here the water was lashed into a milky foam as it tumbled and tore over the rocks on its way to a broader spot quarter of a mile below.

Presently Dick felt his feet touch bottom, but only for an instant. The stream was calmer now, and to one side of the cut he saw a narrow strip of band, leading up to a shelving of rocks, with here and there a tiny brush struggling for existence in a spot which the sunlight never touched. He began to strive with might and main to reach the strip of sand, and finally succeeded. Then he threw himself down, too exhausted to make another move.

"I'm in for it now," he thought, when he somewhat recovered. "How in the world am I ever to get back to that trail again?"

He looked above him. The mountain was high here, and there was nothing resembling a path leading upward. To climb from one scant footing to another would prove perilous, if not impossible.

"We are making a mess of this expedition," he groaned. "First Tom must get lost, or worse, and now I am down here like a rat in a trap. Perhaps we would have been better off if we had never started out."

When Dick felt able he walked from one end of the sand strip to the other. This gave him no satisfaction, and he began to inspect the stream again. Below him was a curve, and what was beyond there was no telling.

"If I enter the water again it may carry me along for miles before I have another chance to get out," he reasoned. "And then I will be just that much further away from Sam and Wumble."

If he had had his pistol he would have fired it to let them know that he was safe, and in the hope that they would come for him. But the weapon had been lost in the tumble down the cliff.

With much hesitation he began to climb up the side of the canyon, making sure that one footing was perfectly safe before he tried another. In this manner he at length reached the height of a hundred feet. He did not dare to look back for fear of tumbling. And yet the path to safety was still a long way off.

"If I can't gain the top and can't go back, what then?" he asked himself, and the cold perspiration stood out on his forehead in beads. There was a bush in front of him, and he squeezed into this, so that he might sit down to consider the situation. Pushed back, the bush suddenly gave way altogether, and to his astonishment Dick fell into the opening of a large cave.

CHAPTER XXV
A CAVE AND A BEAR

"Hullo, here's something new!" thought Dick, as he gathered himself up. Bush and boy had rolled downward for a distance of a dozen feet. He found himself on a rocky floor that was almost level. The cave was ten to twenty feet wide, and so high that in the gloom he could not see the ceiling.

Luckily the boys had with them the waterproof match safes which had proved so handy in Africa, and now Dick brought out the one he carried and lit a match. The bush that had given way was dry, and soon he made of it quite a respectable torch. Satisfied that the cave had no side branches in which he might become lost, he resolved to push into it, in the hope that another opening might present itself, leading to the cliff where the accident had occurred.

The cave was dry and dusty, not a particle of water being anywhere visible. As he walked along he came across some dead leaves and then some small tree branches. These gave him much encouragement, for how could they have gotten into the place if there was no entrance from the mountain side?

Dick had advanced a distance of several hundred yards when he came to a turn to the right, and from this point the bottom of the cave sloped gradually upward. He also made out a glimmer of light, but it was so far off that nothing was to be seen distinctly.

Much encouraged, he pushed on faster than ever, until a line of rocks barred his further progress. He was about to climb the rocks when a growl from a distance caused him to pause.

What was it? With bated breath Dick listened until the growl was repeated. The walls of the cave took it up, and it was repeated over and over again until lost in the distance.

"A bear—or something just as bad!" thought the youth. "Now what's to do?"

He crouched down on the rocks and sat as still as death for fully five minutes. But no further growl reached him, and then he plucked up courage enough to scramble up the rocks, which led to a flooring considerably higher than that over which he had been traveling.

Hurrah! It was the light of day ahead, and Dick could scarcely suppress a shout of joy. But the growl still hung in his mind, and though he went forward it was as silently as a cat and with eyes strained first in one direction and then in another. He was glad he still had the torch, for he remembered that the majority of wild beasts are afraid of a light. It had burned rather low, but by swinging it around he soon started up the blaze.

And now he could see the cave entrance distinctly, less than two hundred feet off. It was low and wide, and there were several bushes growing around it. He started on a run, and as he did so the growl sounded out again, this time almost directly beside him.

He turned swiftly and beheld two glaring eyeballs bent upon him, from the gloom of a hollow on one side of the cave. Whether or not the bear was preparing to leap upon him he could not say, but he jumped like lightning and then tore on as if the demon of the bottomless pit was after him.

The bear was following! Dick knew this without looking behind. The animal was heavy and clumsy, yet it covered the ground with an agility that was surprising. It was hungry, not having tasted meat for several days, and now thought it saw the prospect of a fine meal ahead.

"Back!" yelled Dick, but the animal paid no attention. The boy was running as never before, yet the bear kept drawing closer, until Dick almost felt its hot breath on his neck. He trailed the torch behind him and the beast fell back several paces.

The opening was now gained, and the youth ran out on the mountain side, which was covered with stubble and rocks. Glancing hastily around, Dick saw one rock that was both small and rather high and scrambled to the top of this.

The bear gained the mouth of the cave and looked out suspiciously. Then, as it discovered the boy on the rock, it let out another growl, more terrifying than any which had gone before. Slowly it trotted toward Dick, and then began a circle of the rock, as if to determine whether or not the ground was clear for an attack.

The boy still held the torch, but it was burnt nearly to the end and was in danger of going out every minute. Besides, in the sunshine it did not look half as formidable as it had in the gloomy cave.

Suddenly the bear reared itself up on its hind legs and advanced straight for the rock. At this movement Dick's heart seemed to stop beating. Yet he managed to let out one long scream for help. Then as the bear came still nearer, he thrust the torch end directly into the brute's face.

Of course the animal fell back, and down went the torch on the rocks below, and Dick was now utterly defenseless. The bear appeared to know this, and let out a growl of satisfaction, as though it had its next meal already within its grizzly grasp.

Bang! It was the report of a gun not over a hundred yards away, and the bear dropped to all fours and shook its head wildly. Bang! came another report, and now the bear screamed with pain and fell over on its side. Dick looked behind him in amazement and beheld a stranger on horseback. The stranger had just emptied his double-barreled rifle, and now he came riding up with his pistol in his hand. The bear tried to rise up to meet him, but was too seriously wounded already, and a shot at close range finished the brute's misery.

"Well, young fellow, reckon you was in a putty tight fix?" remarked the stranger, after he had made certain that the animal was dead.

"I was in a tight fix," answered Dick, with a shiver. "You came in the nick of time, and I owe you a good deal for it."

"That's all right—I never go back on a bar if I git a chance at him. But how in thunder came you in such a fix in the fust place?" went on the horseman, who was at least six feet four in height—and about as thin a man as Dick had ever seen.

"It's a long story, sir," was the cautious response. "May I ask who it is that has saved me?"

"Wall, my right handle are James Carson," was the answer. "But them as knows me well callers calls me Slim Jim, and it's good enough fer the likes o' a shadder like me, too, I calkerlate. An' who might you be?"

"I am Dick Rover. I was with my two brothers and an old miner named Jack Wumble when I slipped off my horse into the river over there and nearly lost my life. But I managed to crawl out, and in climbing up the mountain side found yonder cave and came through to this end. In the cave I found the bear and he followed me to here. You know the rest."

"Wall! wall! You have had a narrow escape, youngster, an' no disputin' the p'int. Ef I hadn't a-come as I did, thet air bar would have chawed ye up in no time."

"I know it, Mr. Carson. Your kind—"

"Whoopee, Rover, don't go fer to mister me, or I'll be sorry I killed the bar for ye. I'm plain Slim Jim to all as knows me—Slim Jim the hunter an' trapper. I've spent forty year on these mountains, an' like ez not I'll spend forty more, ef the good Lord allows me to live thet long. An' whar do ye calkerlate your brothers and Jack Wumble air now?"

"I'm sure I don't know. One of my brothers, Tom, got lost and I and Sam and Wumble were looking for him when I had the mishap. Do you know Jack Wumble?"

"Fer sartin I do—knowned him when he war mining up on the ole Bumble Bee Creek, ez he called it."

"Indeed!" cried Dick. "Then perhaps you knew my father, Anderson Rover? He used to be in partnership with a man named Kennedy."

"Knew him—o' course I knew him, lad! An' so you air his son, hey? Wall! wall! shake!" And Slim Jim, as he preferred to be called, thrust forth a hand that was as hard as a piece of horn. But he had a soft heart, and Dick soon learned that he was as much to be trusted as was Jack Wumble.

"I'll do my best to set ye right, lad," said the old hunter, after he had listened to the details of Dick's story. "I think I know about the spot whar ye took the tumble."

Before leaving the vicinity Slim Jim set to work and cut the pelt off the bear and hung it up. He also cut away some of the choicest of the meat.

"It's a pity to leave any o' it behind," he observed. "Some poor folks a-starvin' to deth in the city, an' thar's a meal fer a hundred!"

It was well along in the afternoon when they started, Dick riding behind the old hunter. He felt that he could tell Slim Jim about their mission, and he mentioned how the Baxters were watching them and trying to outwit them.

"I remember thet Baxter, too," said the old hunter. "Wumble kin tell ye how we come nigh to makin' him do a dance on nuthin' onct. I'll take your part agin him every time, hear me!" And his openness showed that he meant what he said.

CHAPTER XXVI
THE BAXTERS TRY TO MAKE TERMS

For the moment after Tom found himself in the presence of the Baxters he could not speak. Then he turned fiercely upon Bill Noxton.

"You have fooled me!" he cried hotly.

"That's right," laughed Noxton sarcastically.

"And let me add, ye was fooled putty easy."

"It's Tom Rover!" ejaculated Dan Baxter, as he leaped to his feet, followed by his parent. "Where did you find him, Noxton; over to that fire?"

"Yes."

"Were the others of the party with him?" put in Arnold Baxter quickly.

"No, he was alone. He got lost from the rest last night, when they gave us the slip in the dark."

"Then you have seen nothing of the others?" said Arnold Baxter, and it was plain to see that he was keenly disappointed.

"No, but I reckon they can't be far off," replied Noxton.

Seeing that Tom contemplated running away, he made the youth dismount. "Better make a prisoner of him," he suggested.

"By all means!" cried Dan Baxter, and brought forth a stout lariat. With this Toni's hands were bound behind him, and his feet were also secured.

"That's number one, Roebuck," laughed Arnold Baxter, turning to the man who had thus far remained silent.

"Tom Rover?" asked the man laconically.

"Yes."

"A bright-looking chap."

"Oh, he's bright enough," growled Baxter senior.

"But it won't help him any," put in Dan, bound to say something.

"Is he the oldest of the three?"

"No, Dick is the oldest. Tom comes next."

"Then it is Dick you ought to have collared," said Roebuck, turning to Noxton.

"I collared the one I happened to see."

"Well, Tom Rover, how do you like your situation?" asked Dan, with a sickly smile, as the men turned away to discuss the situation among themselves.

"Don't like it," replied Tom, as lightly as he could.

"I guess you are sorry, now, that you didn't heed our warning and go back to Gunnison."

"I'm not particularly sorry. I have as much right out here as anybody."

"Oh, you needn't put on airs to me. I know you are trembling in your boots."

"Thanks, but if you'll bring your chin out of the air, Baxter, you'll see that I am wearing shoes."

"Don't you put on airs with me, Tom Rover. You are in our power and you shall suffer for the way you have treated my father and me in the past."

"I have no doubt, Baxter, now I am helpless, that you will do your worst. You were always ready to take an unfair advantage of another."

This answer made Dan Baxter boil with rage, and he stepped closer and shook his fist in Tom's face.

"You be careful or I'll — I'll crack you one," he blustered.

"You're a cheerful brute, Dan, I must say. Why don't you try to fight fair for once? It would be such a delightful change."

"I do fight fair. You and your brothers have no right to poke your noses in my affairs, and my father's."

"This affair out here is our own, not yours. The Eclipse Mine is my father's property."

"And I say it belongs to me and dad," answered Dan, with more force than elegance. "But I won't argue with you. You are in our power and have got to take the consequence."

"What do you intend to do with me?" asked Tom.

"You'll find out soon enough."

"Don't you know that my brothers are in this neighborhood, and that they have the law on their side?"

"Yes, I know your brothers are here—and we'll have them prisoners, too, before long," returned Dan Baxter, and then cut the conversation short by walking away.

Tom had managed to speak bravely enough, yet his heart was by no means light. He realized that the Baxters had not forgotten the past, and that here, in this wild country, they were more inclined than ever to take the law in their own hands.

He was left alone for the best part of an hour, only Noxton seeing to it that he did not run away. Then he was ordered to mount again, his legs being liberated for that purpose.

Feeling it would be foolhardy to refuse, with three men and a boy against him, Tom mounted, and the whole party moved along the mountain to a spot which was evidently well-known to Noxton. Here, at a certain point, was what had once been an overland hotel, but the building was now dilapidated and deserted.

"We'll stop here for the present," said Arnold Baxter grimly. "Get down, Rover," and Tom obeyed.

Inside of the place, two of the rooms were found in fair condition and in one of these Tom was tied fast to a cupboard door. Then the men went out for another parley.

The youth could not hear all that was said, but learned enough to convince him that Al Roebuck, as he was called, was the party who had forged the pardon which had obtained for Arnold Baxter his liberty. For this work Roebuck had been promised a half share in the Eclipse Mine, and of some money which Baxter the elder was hoping to obtain.

At last Arnold Baxter and Dan came in once more and faced Tom.

"Rover, we are now ready to come to terms," began the man.

"Are you ready to release me?"

"Yes—under certain conditions."

"You've got to sign off all rights to that mine," broke in Dan.

"Dan, keep quiet," interposed his father. "I can do this better alone."

"I know him better than you do, dad," returned his graceless son.

"Perhaps, but I am fully capable of making terms with him."

"All right, fire away, I don't care. Only don't let him off too easy."

"I am anxious to settle this matter quietly," went on Arnold Baxter to Tom. "I don't want any more trouble."

"Well, go ahead, I'm listening," came from Tom.

"You are out here to locate a certain mine."

"I don't deny it. The mine belongs to my father."

"It belongs to me—and I am bound to have it."

"You are a jailbird, Mr. Baxter. How can you hold such a property now?"

The criminal winced and clenched his fists.

"Don't be quite so plain-spoken, Rover, it doesn't set well. I say the claim is mine."

"Well?"

"You are in my power."

"Granted."

"Isn't your life worth something to you? To be sure it is. Then why not try to make terms to save it?"

"You are fooling with me. You cannot be it earnest, Arnold Baxter."

"You'll soon see if dad aint in earnest," burst out Dan.

"I am not fooling, Rover, I mean every word of what I say. If you want to save your life you must make terms with me."

"What sort of terms?"

"You must write a letter to your brothers and the man who was with you and get them to return without delay to the East."

"And after that?"

"After they have returned to the East we will set you free, providing you swear to follow them and all of you swear to keep out of Colorado in the future."

"And if I refuse?"

"If you refuse your life shall pay the forfeit," answered Arnold Baxter. "Come now, which do you choose?"

CHAPTER XXVII
DASH FOR LIBERTY

For the minute after Arnold Baxter spoke Tom had nothing to say. The man had offered terms, and if he did not accept them his very life would be in danger.

Now, had Tom been the hero of some dime novel he would have shouted at once, "I refuse your offer — do your worse, base villain that you are!" But being an everyday American boy, with a proper regard for his own life, he revolved the situation in his mind with great care.

"Well, what do you say?" demanded Arnold Baxter impatiently.

"You had better accept dad's offer," broke in Dan.

"I don't know what to say," was the slow answer. "This, you must remember, is brand new to me."

"My offer is a very fair one, Rover. You have gotten yourself in a bad fix, and you can consider yourself lucky if you get out of it with a whole skin."

"If I write the letter, how are you going to deliver it to my two brothers and Jack Wumble?"

"We will find a way."

"And supposing they refuse to go back, what then? I won't be to blame for that."

"They won't refuse — not when they realize that such a refusal means death to you."

"They may. Dick is quite headstrong at times. I don't want to do what I can for you and then suffer anyway."

"Well, if you do your best I will remember it when it comes to a final settlement," responded Arnold Baxter, with more grace than Tom had anticipated.

"Let me think it over for a few hours, and I will give you an answer," said the boy, and though they coaxed and threatened, neither of the Baxters could get any more out of him. At last they left him in disgust, first, however, seeing to it that his bonds were as tight as ever.

As soon as Tom was left alone he looked around for some means by which he might escape from his tormentors. The room was square, with a small window at one side and a broad fireplace at the other. At one end was the door and at the other the cupboard to which he had been fastened.

In his schooldays Tom had been a great hand at doing rope tricks, and when his hands had been tied he had taken care to make his enemies adjust the lariat as loosely as possible. Now, with a dexterous twist or two he cleared his hands, although the effort drew blood on one of his wrists. But, under the circumstances, Tom counted this as nothing.

As soon as he was free the boy tiptoed his way to the window and looked out. He saw Noxton and Roebuck sitting on a fallen tree talking earnestly. Close to the door of the house stood the Baxters, and Arnold Baxter was laying down the law to his son, although what it was all about Tom could not determine.

"I can't go by the window," he mused. "And if I try the door—"

He stopped short, for just then Dan Baxter started to come into the building. But his father stopped him.

"Let the boy alone," cried the elder Baxter. "He'll come around all right, never fear."

"Oh, you're too soft with him," returned the son. "I'd give him a cowhiding." Nevertheless, he walked away, and then all became as silent as before.

Tom realized that whatever was to be done must be done quickly, and walking back he surveyed the broad chimney. It was wide open to the sky, and at one corner of the opening he saw the waving green branch of a tree.

"If I could only get up into the tree," he thought, and no sooner thought than tried. The chimney was dirty, and he was soon covered with soot from head to foot. But being rough the chimney afforded easy footings, and he reached the top without great effort. The tree branch was scarcely two feet from the top.

With great caution the boy peered from the chimney. Noxton and Roebuck were still talking earnestly and both had their backs partly turned in his direction. The Baxters were out of sight.

As quickly as it could be accomplished, Tom stood upon the top of the chimney, caught the tree limb and pulled himself up. The branch swayed violently with his weight, but did not break, and soon he was close to the trunk and out of sight.

"So far so good!" he murmured. "But what shall I do next?"

This question was soon decided. There was another tree close at band, but further from the house than the first, and into this he leaped, and made his way across it to where a drooping branch fell directly over a heavy clump of bushes. Down this branch went Tom and dropped into the bushes as silently as a cat.

It must be confessed that the boy's heart was now thumping like a steam engine. What if he was discovered? He was afraid that his enemies would kill him on the spot.

He looked around and saw the horses tethered among the bushes a hundred feet further on. If only he could gain the animals he felt that escape would be almost secured.

He crawled along the ground like a snake. Once he had to go around a big rock and actually tear his way among the thorns, which scratched him in a dozen places. But behind the rock the shelter was greater, and unable to stand the suspense any longer he set off on a run for his horse.

The animal saw him coming and set up a low whinny of recognition. Then all of the horses swayed around in a bunch, for they were tethered close together.

This gave Tom another idea, and he not only untied his own horse but likewise all of the others. He kept hold of the other lariats as he mounted his steed.

"Get up!" he said sharply but in a low tone, and touched on the flank the horse set off on a gallop, followed by the other animals.

"Hullo, something is wrong with the hosses!" he beard Bill Noxton cry. Then came a rush through the bushes. At the sound Tom bent as low in the saddle as possible and urged his horse to do his best.

"They are stampeding!" came from Arnold Baxter. "Whoa there! whoa!
How did they manage to get loose?"

"The prisoner!" shouted Roebuck. "He is on the leading horse! He has escaped us!"

"Impossible!" gasped the elder Baxter. "Why, I have been watching the house—"

"No matter, it's Tom Rover!" interrupt Dan Baxter. "See, there he goes—and he taking all of our horses with him!"

At this Arnold Baxter drew his pistol and the others also brought forth their firearms. But Tom's steed was not a large one, and while he crouched low in the saddle the horses behind kept his enemies from getting more than an occasional glimpse of him.

On and on went the boy, the horses' hoofs clattering loudly over the rocky trail. The men shouted loudly for him to halt, and several pistol shots rang out, but no damage was done. Soon the enemy was left in the distance.

As soon as he felt that he was safe for the time being, Tom brought his horse down to a walk, in order that he might consider the situation.

Where were the others? That was the all important question. He had escaped from the men who wished him harm, but he was now no better off than when he had fallen in with them.

"But they are a good deal worse off," he thought grimly. "I don't believe they'll want to travel around very far on foot."

It was now sunset, and the youth felt that night would soon be upon him. He did not know which way to turn, although of one thing he was certain—that he wished to keep as far away as possible from those who had held him a prisoner.

Presently he gained the entrance to a small wood, and as it was now too dark to go on he determined to rest for the night. He tied up all of the horses and tried to make himself comfortable at the foot of a large tree. For a long time he could not sleep, but at last he dozed off. His sleep was full of horrible dreams, and his awakening was a rude one.

CHAPTER XXVIII
BILL NOXTON COMES TO GRIEF

"We've found him, boys! Here's the hoss thief, with five o' the hosses with him!"

"Git up thar, young feller, an' give an account o'yerself!"

Tom did not hear these words, but he felt a sharp kick in the ribs and gave a gasp of pain and surprise.

"Let up, Sam," he murmured. "Can't you keep your feet out of my—" He broke off short and stared around him. "Wha—what does this mean?" he stammered.

Three men stood around him-rough-bearded men, each heavily armed.

"It means thet we have collared ye!" answered one of the men sharply. "Git up!" And he kicked Tom again.

"See here, keep your toe to yourself!" cried Tom hotly. "If you are Arnold Baxter's tools you can treat me half decently, anyway," and he leaped up and faced the crowd.

"Who is Arnold Baxter?" questioned the leader of the men quickly.

"I guess you know well enough."

"Oh, all right if you don't want to talk. But let me say, young feller, thet you have got yerself in a fine mess. Don't yer know ez how they hang hoss thieves in these parts?"

"A horse thief! What do you mean? I am no horse thief, if that's what you are driving at."

Tom's straightforward manner appeared to impress all three men. But the leader shrugged his shoulders.

"Ef ye aint no hoss thief, how is it ye hev got all these critters with ye?" he questioned triumphantly.

"I can explain that easily enough. That horse is my own, purchased in Gunnison from Ralph Verbeck the dealer there. Those horses belong to a set of rascals who captured me and made me their prisoner. I got away from them, and to prevent them from following me I took their horses with me."

"Hurmph! Thet's a slick story!"

"It's the plain truth. Do I look like a horse thief?"

"Not persackly, youngster. But two o' them hosses I know well, an' they war stolen. My pards hyer kin prove it."

"Well, I know nothing about that. I have told you the plain truth. You don't claim the horse I said was mine, do you?"

"No. But wot's this tale ye tell of bein' captured?"

Anxious to set himself straight with these men, who appeared to be of upright character, Tom told the larger part of his story, to which the crowd listened patiently. Then they asked him a number of questions.

"I reckon you are O.K.," said the leader at last. "I know Jack Wumble, and I know he wouldn't be attached to a gang that wasn't on the level."

"I don't care what becomes of those horses," went on Tom. "Only I want my own."

"You shall have it, lad. But you must put us on the trail o' them thieves. It runs in my mind thet I know this Bill Noxton, 'though perhaps not by thet handle. Thar used ter be a hoss thief down hyer called Slinky Bill, with a scar on his cheek an' one tooth missin' in front—"

"That's your man. The tooth is still missing and the scar is there as plain as day."

"Then he's the gent as we wants to be introduced to," put in one of the other men.

"I calkerlated he had left these diggin's fer good," added the third newcomer.

"I can try to lead you back to their camp," said Tom, "although I am not altogether sure of the trail. They were stopping at a long, low deserted house, having a wide chimney, and with several big trees growing close by."

"Dillwell's old overland hotel, I'll bet a hoss," cried the leader of the men.

"It must be about ten miles from here," went on Tom.

"Jest about, youngster. Come, we want ye to go with us."

"I will do that willingly, if you'll promise to protect me from the rascals. I suppose they are mad enough to shoot me down on sight."

"We'll see ye through—ef everything is straight," answered Hank Yates, for such was the name of the leading spirit of the party.

The men had their own horses close at hand, and soon all were in the saddle, with the extra horses bringing up the rear, as before. The men had rations with them, and offered Tom some crackers and a bit of meat as they progressed.

They were not a bad crowd, although very rough and stern, and it developed presently that Hank Yates had known the Kennedy who had been Anderson Rover's partner in mining operations.

"He war a good man," said Yates. "A banrup, whole-souled critter. It's a pity he had to turn up his toes, with wuss men hangin' on an never dyin', at all."

Half of the distance to the old hotel had been covered, when on coming out on a little hill one of the men called attention to a man and a boy riding along the top of a ridge, a short distance away.

"It's my brother Sam and Jack Wumble!" ejaculated Tom. "Oh, but am I not glad to see them again!"

He set up a shout and waved his cap, and soon Wumble saw him and waved his hand in return. Then the old miner and Sam came forward at top speed.

"Tom!" came from Sam, and he rode up close and almost embraced his brother. "Where in the world have you been?"

"Been with the enemy," answered Tom. "I can tell you I paid up for going to sleep on the trait!" he added half comically. The meeting made his heart ten times lighter than it had been.

"Where is Dick?"

"Thet's the wust on it," answered Wumble. "Dick had a dirty tumble, and we can't find him nowhar."

Of course the stories on both sides had to be told. Jack Wumble could not keep from laughing when told that Tom had been mistaken for a horse thief.

"Not but wot ye run away with them hosses slick enough," he added slyly.

Dick's disappearance sobered Tom greatly.

"Can it be possible that he has been drowned?" he asked.

"I crawled down to the river, but couldn't find hide nor hair of him," answered Wumble.

Soon all were on the way to the old hotel. As they drew closer Yates warned them to be cautious.

"Perhaps we can do a bit o' surprisin'," he explained.

"Here comes Noxton!" exclaimed Tom.

"Slinky Bill, sure enough," returned Yates, and one of his companions nodded.

Noxton was still fifty feet away when he saw them, and gave a shout of consternation. Then he turned and tried to run away.

"Stop!" called Hank Yates. "Stop, or I'll fire on ye!"

But instead of stopping Noxton ran the faster. Seeing this, the man of the plains raised his pistol, took steady aim, and fired. Noxton was hit in the leg and went down in a heap, shrieking with pain.

CHAPTER XXIX
LOCATING THE LOST MINE

While Yates and another of the men ran toward Noxton to make him a prisoner, the others turned their attention to the Baxters and Al Roebuck.

The Baxters were hiding behind a clump of bushes, but now, as soon as discovered, they took to their heels, making sure that the bushes and trees should keep them screened, so that there would be no danger from a fire such as had brought down their unlucky companion.

"They're on us, dad!" groaned Dan Baxter, "Oh, why did we ever come out here!"

"Silence, Dan," whispered Arnold Baxter. "If we don't keep still they may shoot us down in cold blood." And then Dan became as mum as an oyster, although his teeth chattered with terror.

On went father and son, down a hill and into a deep valley where the rocks were numerous and the growth thick. Several shots flew over their heads, causing Dan to almost drop from heart failure.

"I—I can't ru—run much further!" he panted.

"Come, here is an opening between the rocks," whispered Arnold Baxter. "In you go, before it is too late. If they follow us, we can sell our lives as dearly as possible."

Dan gave a groan at this, and slipped into the hollow. He did not wish to sell his life at any price.

"Let us put out a—a flag of truce," he whined. "Give them everything, father, but don't let them shoot us!" Every ounce of courage had oozed away from him, for he had seen Noxton brought down, and thought the rascal was dead.

"Shut up, you softy!" answered his parent in a rage. "Shut up, and we will be safe. I'll never give in to a Rover," he added vehemently.

Tom and Sam had gone after the Baxters, with Jack Wumble behind them while the last man of the party turned to collar Roebuck. But Roebuck was game, and fired at his assailant, who fired in return, and each man was slightly wounded in the shoulder. Then Roebuck disappeared in the woods back of the old hotel, and that was the last seen of him for the time being.

The hunt for the Baxters was kept up until nearly nightfall. But they remained in hiding, and although Tom and Sam passed within fifty feet of the hollow, they were not discovered.

"They have given us the slip," said Tom, "It's too bad! I thought we had them, sure!"

As soon as the search was over it was discovered that two of the horses were missing. The several pistol shots had frightened them away, and in the gathering darkness they could not be located.

The entire party camped that night in the old hotel, and Tom showed where he had been a prisoner, and how he had escaped up the chimney. Noxton was not dangerously wounded, and the men did what they could to allay the pain he was suffering. Yet they had little sympathy for him, for, as stated before, horse stealing in that locality was considered one of the worst of crimes.

"But we'll take ye back to the county seat," said Yates. "And ye shall have a fair trial."

"Take all I have, but let me go!" pleaded Noxton, but to this the men with Yates would not listen. Early in the morning the party under Yates set off, taking Noxton along, although the criminal protested that he was too weak to ride. It may be as well to add here that, later on, Noxton, alias Slinky Bill, was tried in court and given a sentence of five years for his misdeeds.

Jack Wumble and Sam had brought along Dick's horse, and they now took good care that the animal should not get away from them. Where to look for Dick, however, was a poser.

"Well, I'll tell you one thing," Tom declared, "I'm not going on to Larkspur Creek until he is found."

"Or until we have found out what has become of him," added Sam. "He may be dead, you know."

"I reckon we had best go back to where he took his tumble," said Wumble. "If he escaped he'll come back thar himself, more'n likely."

This appeared to be good advice, and an hour after the departure of Yates and the others they mounted and set off.

Less than half a mile had been covered when, of a sudden, there came a shot, and a bullet cut through the brush beside them.

"Hullo! this won't do!" cried the old miner. "Come out of sight, an' be putty quick about it, too!"

They rode into a patch of wood and halted. But no more shots came, nor could they locate that which had been fired.

"One thing is certain, at least one of yer enemies is a-watching of us," was the old miner's comment. "We'll keep behind shelter after this." And they did.

It was hard traveling, and poor Sam was utterly worn out by the time the trail along the watercourse was again reached.

"I've got to let up a bit," he murmured. "I can't sit up in the saddle any more!"

"I shouldn't have pushed ye so hard," answered Wumble sympathetically. "If ye—" he stopped short. "Who's that?"

He dodged behind a rock, and the others did the same. Somebody was stirring below them, in the timber. All drew their pistols.

"If it's an enemy we'll give them as good as they send," said Tom, and he meant it.

But it was not the enemy; it was Dick, and he soon appeared and called to them. They were overjoyed, and ran out to meet him and Slim Jim, his companion. There was hearty handshaking all around. Then as they rested each told his tale. It was such a happy gathering as is not easily forgotten.

"You couldn't have fallen in with a better man nor Slim Jim," said Jack Wumble to Dick. "He's got the warmest heart in all Colorady, he has!"

It was decided to wait until the morrow before setting out again for Larkspur Creek. Slim Jim agreed to accompany them, for to the hunter and trapper one spot in the mountains was about as good as another.

"An' I'll help ye keep an eye open for them Baxters," said the old hunter.

A good night's rest did wonders for all hands, and they were stirring bright and early. Slim Jim knew every foot of the way, and he told Wumble of a short cut to the creek which was even better to travel than the short trail the old miner had selected.

For two days the party went on, over hills and mountains and across marvelous canyons and valleys, thick with pines and firs. The boys had never seen such scenery, and for the time being their enemies were forgotten.

Late in the afternoon of the second day they came out on the side of a low mountain which overlooked Larkspur Creek.

"Here we are at the Larkspur at last," cried Jack Wumble.

"And how far still to Kennedy's claim, do you think?" asked Dick eagerly.

"Not more than two or three miles. We'll have to hunt up the landmarks," answered the old miner, but hunting landmarks had to be deferred to the next day. Then they set about it in earnest, and by noon they were on the same ground which Anderson Rover's mining partner had traveled so many years before.

They were trying to put down the first of their stakes when a pistol shot rang out, and Dick received a slight wound in the hand. Looking up the mountain side they saw Arnold Baxter's savage face gazing down at them. Behind the father was his son Dan, and close by stood Roebuck. Evidently their enemies meant to fight for the possession of the mine to the bitter end.

CHAPTER XXX
THE LANDSLIDE—CONCLUSION

"Dick, are you badly hurt?" cried Tom.

"No—it's only a scratch. But it was a close call."

"To cover!" came from Jack Wumble. "Quick, all of you!"

There was no need to call out, for all realized that they were in a dangerous position. It was Arnold Baxter who fired on Dick. Now Tom fired in return, and so true was his aim that the elder Baxter was hit in the left shoulder.

As soon as our friends were under cover they held a council of war.

"We ought to round 'em up," muttered Jack Wumble. "Don't you think so, Jim?"

"I am with ye on it," answered the old trapper. "We air five to three, although one o' the crowd is wounded."

"It's not much—only a scratch," said Dick, as he showed the wound. "Yes, let us surround them if we can. Anyway, it will be better if we get on the high ground above them. It's useless to think of staking off the claim while they are in the vicinity. They'll pull up our stakes, and shoot us in the bargain."

Their talk was interrupted by a crashing of the bushes, and looking up they saw that their enemies were beginning to roll rocks down toward them. One rock, weighing several tons, tumbled within two yards of them.

"All right, we'll try some o' that when we're on top," said Slim Jim.

It had threatened rain, and now the drops began to come down, at first scatteringly, and then in a steady downpour. In this rain they moved off through the brush, leading their horses and following the old hunter, who knew more of the old Indian trails than did even Jack Wumble.

It was necessary to make a long detour, for the rocks at one point were so steep that mounting them was all out of the question. This took them an eighth of a mile to the northward of the claim.

It was now raining so hard that the water seemed to come down in sheets, and they felt compelled to seek temporary shelter. It had also begun to lightning, and the thunder roared and rumbled among the mountains in a manner that was deafening.

"This is about as bad as that tornado we encountered in Africa," observed Sam, as he crouched close to his brothers. "Don't you remember it and how the lightning struck that baobab tree?"

Yes, both remembered it well. "It was awful," said Tom. "I hope the lightning doesn't come near us here."

If anything, the rain now came down heavier than before, until Jack Wumble declared it to be the greatest downpour he had ever witnessed in that section of the country. The water leaped over the rocks in tiny waterfalls, and soon Larkspur Creek became a raging torrent. The sky was inky black, and they could not see a dozen paces in any direction.

Suddenly a strange rumble reached their ears, a rumble that made both Wumble and Slim Jim turn pale and look at each other with faces full of fear. The rumble rose and fell, shaking the earth beneath them, and mingling with a grinding and crashing and ripping that seemed to strike each one to the very heart.

"What is it? The end of the world?" gasped Sam.

"A landslide," answered Wumble. "Please God, it doesn't come this way!"

They waited, and the next half-minute seemed an eternity. The ground continued to tremble beneath them, and the rumble kept coming closer and closer. "We are doomed!" wailed Tom, but then the rumble and crashing passed them by and was slowly lost in the distance, until with one last crash it came to a sudden end.

"It's over!" said Slim Jim. "Thank Heaven, we escaped it!"

"You are sure it was a landslide?" asked Dick, when he felt able to speak.

"Yes, my lad, and a putty big one, too. Somewhar along this mountain side you will find a furrow cut down to the creek, an' find thet tons an' tons o' stone and dirt have slid down fer quarter o' a mile or more. Perhaps the slide has filled up the creek entirely."

The rain continued to come down, now drowning out every other sound. But wet as it was, Wumble urged that they go still higher up the mountain, to escape any other landslide that might be imminent.

So up they toiled until a large table rock was gained. At this point a second rock gave them shelter, and here they remained throughout the whole of one of the most disagreeable nights the Rover boys had ever encountered.

The storm and the landslide had driven away all thoughts of surrounding the Baxters and Roebuck, but with the coming of morning the skies cleared, and they felt as if they must do as originally planned.

"Unless the landslide paid 'em off," said Jack Wumble.

"Do you think they were caught in it?" asked Dick.

"No tellin', lad, until we locate the slide."

To locate the landslide was not difficult, since it had passed to their right. They soon made out its trail, which moved down to the creek in a zigzag fashion. Sure enough the creek was partly filled with the debris, and here the opposite bank was overflowed to the extent of several acres.

"We may find some rich deposits down thar," said Wumble. "A landslide sometimes provides a harvest for prospectors."

They moved on cautiously until they came to the spot where the Baxters and Roebuck had been seen last. Here the landslide had been at its worst, and rocks and trees had been torn up and cast down as by a giant's hand. Not a trace of the enemy was to be discovered, until Jack Wumble at last made out a part of a man's coat lying a hundred feet away. They ran to the spot, and soon uncovered the lifeless form of Roebuck. The man had been literally mauled to death by the fury of the elements.

"Poor fellow!" murmured Tom, as he gazed at the remains. "It was a dreadful death to die!"

"Yes, and he probably wasn't prepared for it," said Dick soberly. "I wonder if the Baxters were caught, too?"

"More'n likely," put in Wumble. "Look, here is a man's hat."

"Arnold Baxter's hat," cried Tom. "I noted it particularly when I was their prisoner. Where can the man be?"

"There are tons an' tons o' loose dirt just be low here," said Slim Jim. "Ye see the ground turned over and over as it rolled. Probably both o' the Baxters are under that dirt, mebbe twenty or thirty foot down."

At this all of the Rover boys shuddered. Very likely the old hunter spoke the truth. What a terrible fate for their old enemies!

"Let us go away," whispered Sam. "I can't stand this any longer!" And he rushed off with the tears standing in his eyes. The others were also affected, and glad enough to leave the place, once and forever. Wumble and Slim Jim threw Roebuck's body into a hollow and placed some dirt over it, and then built up a little mound of stones to mark the spot.

It was not until the next day that the party returned to the creek and began to look up the Eclipse Mine once more. The landslide had cut across this, and it was not long before both Wumble and Slim Jim declared the ground to be full of good paying "dirt," to use their own term. The claim was staked out to the boys' satisfaction, and then Wumble staked out a claim just above Discovery, as it is called in mining laws, while Slim Jim staked out one for himself just below Discovery. All three claims ran to both sides of the creek, so that no one would suffer for water when mining operations should begin.

"And those claims will yield us thousands of dollars!" said Jack Wumble. "Boys, we will all be rich."

"Hurrah!" shouted Tom. "I'm glad I came West, after all."

"And so am I," said Sam. "Dick, what do you say?"

"I say hurrah for the Eclipse Mine, and all the gold it will bring us," answered Dick. "Won't father be pleased when he learns the news?"

Here let us bring to a close the story of the Rover boys' trip out West. They had faced many grave perils, but one after another these perils had been surmounted, and now, when success had finally crowned their efforts, all the hardships were forgotten.

In due course of time the title to the Eclipse Mine was established in law, and later on Anderson Rover sent out a body of skilled miners to work the claim for all it was worth. It proved to be as valuable as anticipated, and the Rovers were, of course, correspondingly happy.

The claims staked out by Jack Wumble and by Slim Jim proved also to be good payers from the start.

When the boys got home they found that the story of the Baxters' fate had preceded them. Many folks were inclined to think that the wrongdoers deserved the catastrophe which had overtaken them. As nothing was heard of either father or son for a long while, it was presumed that both were dead beyond a doubt.

But they were not dead, although terribly bruised and unable to do much for themselves for a long while. The landslide threw both into the creek, and when they came to their senses they were fully a mile from the scene of the disaster. Here they fell in with a body of miners from Canada, and these men took them to a settlement still further West, where Arnold Baxter hovered between life and death for many weeks. Dan recovered more quickly.

"It's the Rovers' fault," growled Dan Baxter, when he was able to sit up. "I'll fix them yet."

He had still many plans for the future, and what some of them were will be told in the next volume of the series, to be entitled "The Rover Boys on the Great Lakes; or, The Secret of the Island Cave." In this volume we will meet all of our old friends again, and also learn what was done by the Rover boys to outwit their old enemy.

Yet all went well for the present. Randolph Rover had quite recovered, so the boys' Aunt Martha was happy. Anderson Rover could now walk around again as well as ever.

"Never saw such boys in my life!" declared Martha Rover. "No matter what scrape they get into, they always come out with colors flying. God bless 'em every one!"

And to this, kind reader, let us say Amen, and bid each other good-by.

THE END